TOPSHAM LIBRARY
TEL: 01392 874955
07. AUG 06
WITHDRAWN
FROM
DEVON LIBRARY SERVICES

D11391306 X 0 100

A Journey around my Room

and

A Nocturnal Expedition around my Room

Xavier de Maistre

Translated by Andrew Brown

ET REMOTISSIMA PROPE

Hesperus Classics

Hesperus Classics
Published by Hesperus Press Limited
4 Rickett Street, London SW6 1RU
www.hesperuspress.com

A Journey around my Room first published in French in 1795;
A Nocturnal Expedition around my Room first published in French in 1825;
This translation first published by Hesperus Press Limited, 2004
Reprinted 2006

Designed and typeset by Fraser Muggeridge
Printed in Jordan by Jordan National Press

ISBN: 1-84391-099-3

CONTENTS

FOREWORD

In the spring of 1790, a twenty-seven-year-old Frenchman, Xavier de Maistre, undertook a journey around his bedroom, later entitling the account of what he had seen *A Journey around my Room.* Gratified by his experiences, in 1798, de Maistre undertook a second journey. This time, he travelled by night and ventured out as far as the window ledge, later entitling his account *A Nocturnal Expedition around my Room.*

Xavier de Maistre was born in 1763 in the picturesque town of Chambéry at the foot of the French Alps. He was of an intense, romantic nature, was fond of reading, especially Montaigne, Pascal and Rousseau, and of paintings, especially Dutch and French domestic scenes. At the age of twenty-three, de Maistre became fascinated by aeronautics. Etienne Montgolfier had, three years before, achieved international renown by constructing a balloon that flew for eight minutes above the royal palace at Versailles, bearing as passengers a sheep called Montauciel (Climb-to-the-sky), a duck and a rooster. De Maistre and a friend constructed a pair of giant wings out of paper and wire and planned to fly to America. They did not succeed. Two years later de Maistre secured himself a place in a hot-air balloon and spent a few moments floating above Chambéry before the machine crashed into a pine forest.

Then in 1790, while he was living in a modest room at the top of an apartment building in Turin, de Maistre pioneered a mode of travel that was to make his name: room-travel.

Introducing *A Journey around my Room*, Xavier's brother, the political theorist Joseph de Maistre, emphasised that it was not Xavier's intention to cast aspersions on the heroic deeds of the great travellers of the past, Magellan, Drake, Anson and Cook. Magellan had discovered a western route to the Spice Islands around the southern tip of South America, Drake had circumnavigated the globe, Anson had produced accurate sea charts of the Philippines and Cook had confirmed the existence of a southern continent. 'They were no doubt remarkable men,' wrote Joseph; it was just that his brother had discovered a way of travelling that might be infinitely more practical for those neither as brave nor as wealthy as they.

'Thousands of people who, before I came along, had never dared to travel, and others who had not been able to, and yet others who had never even dreamed of travelling, will be emboldened to do so by my example,' explained Xavier as he prepared for his journey. 'Would even the most indolent of men hesitate to set off with me in search of a pleasure that will cost him neither effort nor money?' He particularly recommended room-travel to the poor and to those afraid of storms, robberies and high cliffs.

The story is a giant proverbial shaggy dog. De Maistre locks his door and changes into his dressing gown. Without the need for luggage, he travels to the sofa, the largest piece of furniture in the room. His journey having shaken him from his usual lethargy, he looks at it through fresh eyes and rediscovers some of its qualities. He admires the elegance of its feet and remembers the pleasant hours he has spent cradled in its cushions, dreaming of love and advancement in his career. From his sofa, de Maistre spies his bed. Once again, from a traveller's vantage point, he learns to appreciate this complex piece of furniture. He feels grateful for the nights he has spent in it and takes pride in the aptness of the colour of his bed. 'I... advise any man who can do so to have a pink and white bed,' he writes, for these are colours to induce calm and pleasant reveries in the fragile sleeper.

De Maistre's work springs from a profound and suggestive insight: that the pleasure we derive from journeys is perhaps dependent more on the mindset with which we travel than on the destination we travel to. If only we could apply a travelling mindset to our own locales, we might find these places becoming no less interesting than the high mountain passes and jungles of South America.

What then is a travelling mindset? Receptivity might be said to be its chief characteristic. We approach new places with humility. We carry with us no rigid ideas about what is interesting. We irritate locals because we stand on traffic islands and in narrow streets and admire what they take to be strange small details. We risk getting run over because we are intrigued by the roof of a government building or an inscription on a wall. We find a supermarket or hairdresser's unusually fascinating. We dwell at length on the layout of a menu or the clothes of the presenters on the evening news. We are alive to the layers of history beneath the present and take notes and photographs.

Home, on the other hand, finds us more settled in our expectations. We feel assured that we have discovered everything interesting about a neighbourhood, primarily by virtue of having lived there a long time. It seems inconceivable that there could be anything new to find in a place which we have been living in for a decade or more. We have become habituated and therefore blind.

De Maistre tried to shake us from our passivity. In his second volume of room-travel, *A Nocturnal Expedition around my Room*, he went to his window and looked up at the night sky. Its beauty made him frustrated that such ordinary scenes were not more generally appreciated: 'How few people… are now enjoying with me the sublime spectacle that the heavens spread out, in vain, for drowsy men!… Those who actually are asleep are one thing; but what would it cost those people out for a stroll, or those others emerging in crowds from the theatre, to look up for a moment and admire the brilliant constellations that are shining down on their heads from every direction?'

The reason they weren't looking was that they had never done so before. They had fallen into the habit of considering their universe to be boring – and it had duly fallen into line with their expectations. We meet people who have crossed deserts, floated on icecaps, and cut their way through jungles – and yet in whose souls we would search in vain for evidence of what they have witnessed. Wrapped in his dressing gown, satisfied by the confines of his own bedroom, Xavier de Maistre was gently nudging us to try, before taking off for distant hemispheres, to notice what we have already seen.

– Alain de Botton, 2004

INTRODUCTION

There is a man alone in a room. Maybe he doesn't know how he got there, and starts to find the whole of his previous existence baffling, his memories of life outside the room tenuous and incoherent, his own sense of self-identity fraught and enigmatic: he could be one of the heroes of Beckett's *Trilogy*. Sometimes the man has been wandering through 'the wilderness of this world' and has lighted in a certain place where he goes to sleep, and dreams of the City of Destruction and the path that leads from it, through Vanity Fair and past Doubting Castle, to the Celestial City: Bunyan's Pilgrim. Another man living alone in a room also goes to sleep, and sees his home town of Combray, and high-society life in Paris, and apple trees on a rainy spring day in Normandy: Proust's Narrator. (Perhaps the *real* last words of *In Search of Lost Time,* accidentally omitted in all existing editions, are: 'So I awoke, and behold it was a dream.')

The ideas that visit a man in a room can have momentous implications. On 10th November 1619, a soldier returning to the army of Duke Maximilian of Bavaria from the coronation of Ferdinand II in Frankfurt was detained by the harsh winter weather and took up quarters near Ulm, in a room with a stove, where he found the leisure to think through some of the metaphysical perplexities that had been preoccupying him: the soldier was Descartes, and the result of his wintry, room-bound ponderings was the *Cogito*, expressing in a nutshell a new epoch in philosophy.

Xavier de Maistre's *A Journey around my Room* and its successor, *A Nocturnal Expedition,* are akin to all these. Like Molloy and Malone and other of Beckett's almost immobilised but unstoppably loquacious protagonists, de Maistre finds that isolation from society, and the relative absence of stimuli from the world outside, lead him to question his identity (though in a much more relaxed and debonair way than in Beckett), make him reflect on the unstable flux of experience that the practical needs of 'ordinary' life tend to conceal, and force him to supplement the paucity of events in the room by resorting to memory, imagination, daydream and storytelling – which sometimes seem to merge into one another. The dimensions of the room vary in accordance with his subjective moods: sometimes the four walls are a little claustrophobic, but more often the room suddenly turns out to be vast in its dimensions, as if the distance from his armchair to his desk suddenly constituted a vast and almost uncrossable terrain (shades of Beckett again: and anyone who has ever suffered post-viral fatigue will know just how he feels).

Like Bunyan, de Maistre euphemises his time in the room; like Bunyan, he was in fact imprisoned there (de Maistre was confined to house arrest for forty-two days over a duelling incident). There is little of Bunyan's evangelising fervour in de Maistre's dreams and visions, and yet in his work too there is a 'city of destruction' in the background: the Paris of the French Revolution. Xavier de Maistre was the brother of that Prince of Reactionaries, Joseph de Maistre, whose writings (which Baudelaire, with a degree of irony that is difficult to judge, and quite possibly without any irony at all, claimed had 'taught him how to reason') promoted an unflinching Papal absolutism, a stubborn monarchism, and a hair-raising cult of the sacramental significance of the death penalty (in the specific shape of the executioner), as the only authentic response to the ills of modernity. Xavier was less systematic in his politics than Joseph, but the charm of the *Journey* goes hand in hand with his conviction that Paris had, as a result of the events following 1789, become the capital city of the Antichrist, which he can contemplate with horrified fascination from the (relatively) safe haven of Turin. And Xavier's apparently desultory meditations not only turn his room (his prison) into the launching pad for some understated but insistent political opinions (quite the opposite of Bunyan's, of course); they also turn the microcosm of his seclusion into a macrocosm that ranges in epic (or mock-epic) style through time and space, and incidentally (and somewhat unexpectedly) fosters some favourable comments on that very unreactionary but equally exploratory character, the Satan of Bunyan's contemporary, Milton.

Like Proust's Narrator, de Maistre finds that enclosure within four walls is a necessary precondition for writing about the life he lived outside them; and like Descartes, he concocts his own (much more whimsical) philosophical system, delightfully brief and refreshingly devoid of metaphysical angst (see chapter 16 of the *Expedition*).

On a rather more sustained note, he indulges in a fanciful reprise of Cartesian dualism, which is given different forms in the *Journey* and the *Nocturnal Expedition*: the experience of being alone will naturally tend to lead to an obsession with 'reflection' (indeed, in the *Journey*, with mirrors) and with the sense of doubling that is forced on anyone who can think but not act, or is obliged, for company, to talk to himself. (A paradoxical idea: when we talk to ourselves, who is doing the talking and who is doing the listening?) But then, in all these cases, solitude in a room leads above all to writing, which is almost as odd (can I write without also reading?).

And what do you write about, from inside your room? Both the *Journey* and the *Expedition* oscillate between inside and outside – between examining the author's immediate environment and speculating about, or remembering, or anticipating what lies beyond it. An enumeration of the things in one's room can be highly instructive. Nothing is more taken for granted, and yet nothing can say more about who we are than the things with which we have surrounded ourselves. De Maistre, being under house arrest, uses his enforced solitude to contemplate the artefacts and commodities around him, and makes them strange. All that was close – so close as to be almost invisible – becomes far: becomes, at times, a pretext for imaginative fugues that lead in all sorts of unpredictable directions.

De Maistre has had several successors in the art of 'travelling around your room': two of the more recent and most illustrious are Daniel Spoerri and Georges Perec. Spoerri's *An Anecdoted Topography of Chance* is a highly complex text which weaves commentaries of almost Talmudic detail around the objects lying at random (in so far as anything *is* random) on the table in his room, which thus become the pretext for associations of ideas, chains of memory, stories and anecdotes which in turn bristle with footnotes, and footnotes on footnotes, that mimic such earlier 'encyclopedic' works as the seventeenth-century *Critical Dictionary* of Pierre Bayle. It is also faithful to the spirit of de Maistre in its digressions and parenthetical remarks and general indifference to the straight line which (as Doctor Who and other sages have observed) may be the shortest way of getting from one point to another but is not necessarily the most interesting.

(De Maistre pays explicit homage to another great exponent of the squiggle and the diversion and the sudden flight of fancy, also mentioned by Spoerri: the Sterne of both *Tristram Shandy* and that 'journey' that does indeed travel, but despite its title – *A Sentimental Journey through France and Italy* – characteristically never gets any further than Lyons.)

And Perec too refuses to indulge in contempt for what is familiar, and is happy (and sometimes alarmed) to find infinite space in a nutshell. His manic attention to the world's visible surfaces, his love of objects – both as things and as the bearers of rich and mysterious meanings – is often brought to bear on his most immediate working environment. In *Espèces d'espaces* (literally, 'types of spaces') he meditates on the page on which he is writing, and then moves out successively to the bed (where, among other things, he has spent so much time reading), the bedroom, the apartment, the block, the street, the town, Europe, the world, space. This is reminiscent of de Maistre's flights of cosmic fancy winging out from the confines of his cell, though de Maistre has none of Perec's more sociological obsession with classification (how do we define the different spaces in which we live, and how are they related to one another?). Perec's *Penser/Classer* ('Thinking/Classifying') foregrounds in its very title these more theoretical concerns, and at times restricts itself to an even smaller topography than his room – like Spoerri, he notes the objects that are on his worktable (the lamp, the ashtray, several stones, a lump of lead, etc. – though, as he comments, if you *are* going to make a list, you must try your best to avoid the amnesia and impatience of an 'etc.') and ponders on the possibility of writing the history of some of them – how they came to be there, and what they might say about his habits or his changing tastes. This is similar to de Maistre's cataloguing of the paintings on his walls – though again, there is a downbeat and ruminative tone to de Maistre which is quite different from Perec's probing, intense, high-voltage gaze, obsessed with not leaving anything out, not forgetting a single thing: after all, the history from which Perec emerged – he came from a Jewish family, his father died in the early days of the Second World War, his mother was deported and almost certainly perished in Auschwitz – forced him to cling with grim tenacity to *everything*, since once you start forgetting a single detail, you are yielding to an amnesia that might swallow up even the most tragic and momentous events, such as the Shoah.

And this may put de Maistre's *Journey* and *Expedition* in a slightly different light. It would, of course, be a shame to deprive them of the 'charm' which many readers have quite rightly found in them. But like all those other men in rooms, writing about the things around them and using them as pretexts for ever-expanding musings, de Maistre is, after all, *in reality* 'cabined, cribbed, confined'. They are all prisoners (of time and history as well as space), forced to use their imagination to transcend the claustrophobia of their condition: by turning their gaze to their immediate environment, are they looking for a key to help them escape, or are they so resigned to confinement that they are content merely, as it were, to decorate the walls of their prison cells? The question as posed sets up a false antithesis: maybe a close and scrupulous attention to the prison cell (or 'the world') is a way of escaping it, or a precondition for some change in circumstances that would be tantamount to an escape. But all these writers make us reflect on the extent to which writing both connects with the world (the 'outside') and holds it at bay; can be both social – think of de Maistre's kindness, however hedged about with the ironies of Shandean sentimentalism it may be, and the way he always seems to be *addressing* someone – and solitary, longing for a reality to which it constantly refers while at the same time dallying with the idea that its own imaginative musings may ultimately be more satisfactory (and perhaps even more real). The journey around your room may be as good as any trip around that slightly bigger but equally finite room, the world. De Maistre is glad to leave house arrest at the end of the *Journey*, but already nostalgic, too, for the liberty it gave him – and all too happy to return, in the nocturne of the *Expedition*, to an exploration of that inner space. For the apparent inwardness and retreat of writing (what Erich Heller called 'the artist's journey into the interior') may paradoxically be a better way of exploring, not just the great outdoors (hence the plethora of cultural references in de Maistre's text), but a quite different dimension as well: the Great Outside.

– Andrew Brown, 2004

Note on the Text:

I have used the texts in Xavier de Maistre, *Voyage autour de ma chambre*, Collection des Cent Chefs-d'Oeuvre (Paris: Robert Laffont, 1959). See also Daniel Spoerri, *An Anecdoted Topography of Chance*, translated by Emmett Williams with additional material by Dieter Roth and illustrations by Topor, Atlas Arkhive Four: Documents of the Avant-Garde no. 4 (London: Atlas Press, 1995). The texts I mentioned by Perec are translated in Georges Perec, *Species of Spaces and Other Pieces*, translated by John Sturrock (London: Penguin, 1997).

A Journey around my Room

1

In many a deep author of wisdom quite sublime
I've read that too much travelling is an utter waste of time.
Vert-Vert[1]

What a splendid thing it is to embark on a new career, and to appear all of a sudden before the world of learning holding a book, in the same way that an unexpected comet flashes through space!

No, I will no longer keep my book to myself; here it is, gentlemen: read it. I have undertaken and completed a forty-two-day journey around my room. The interesting observations I have made, and the continual pleasure I experienced en route, filled me with the desire to publish it; the certainty of being useful was the decisive factor. My heart senses an inexpressible satisfaction when I think of the countless unhappy people to whom I am here offering a sure and certain resource against boredom, and an alleviation of the ills they endure. The pleasure you find in travelling around your room is safe from the restless jealousy of men; it is independent of the fickleness of fortune.

After all, is there any person so unhappy, so abandoned, that he doesn't have a little den into which he can withdraw and hide away from everyone? Nothing more elaborate is needed for the journey.

I am sure that any sensible man will adopt my system, whatever kind of character he may have, and whatever his temperament; whether he be stingy or prodigal, rich or poor, whether he was born in a torrid zone or near the Pole, he can travel just as I do; finally, in the immense family of men who swarm over the surface of the world, there isn't a single one – no, not one (I mean of those who live in rooms) who will, after having read this book, be disinclined to endorse the new way of travelling that I am introducing into the world.

2

I could start to sing the praises of my journey by saying that it cost me nothing; and this fact deserves to be pointed out. It means that it will straight away be lauded and fêted by those of middling wealth; and there is another class of men with whom it will be even more popular, for this same reason that it costs nothing. – 'And who can they be?' – Ah, you mean you have to ask? Rich people, of course! Furthermore, what a grand resource this way of travelling will be for the sick! They won't need to fear the inclemency of the air and the seasons. – As for the cowardly, they will be safe from robbers; they will encounter neither precipices nor quagmires. Thousands of people who, before I came along, had never dared to travel, and others who had not been able to, and yet others who had never even dreamed of travelling, will be emboldened to do so by my example. Would even the most indolent of men hesitate to set off with me in search of a pleasure that will cost him neither effort nor money? So, buck up then: let's be off! – Follow me, all you who, because of some mortification of love, or a negligent friend, have been keeping to your apartments, far from the pettiness and perfidy of men. Let all the unhappy, sick and bored people of the whole world follow me! – Let all the lazy arise en masse! And you whose minds are brooding over sinister plans to reform your way of life or retire from it as a result of some infidelity; you who, in some boudoir, have renounced the world for good; you amiable anchorites of an evening, come along too. Take my word for it and leave those dark ideas behind; you are wasting time which you could be spending enjoying yourselves, and you are not thereby gaining any time for wisdom: be so good as to accompany me on my journey; we will travel in short marches, laughing all along the way at the travellers who have seen Rome and Paris; – no obstacle will be able to stop us; and, yielding merrily to our imagination, we will follow it wherever it pleases to lead us.

3

There are so many curious people in the world! – I'm convinced that everyone would like to know why my journey around my room lasted forty-two days instead of forty-three, or any other space of time; but how can I tell the reader since I myself don't know? All I can vouch for is that, if the work is too long for his liking, I wasn't in any position to make it any shorter; all traveller's vanity apart, I'd have been happy with a single chapter. I was, admittedly, in my room, with all the pleasure and comfort possible; but, alas! I wasn't free to leave it as and when I wished; I even think that, without the mediation of certain powerful persons who took an interest in my fate, and for whom my gratitude still glows strong, I would have had plenty of time to bring forth an entire folio volume, so greatly were the protectors who made me travel in my room disposed in my favour!

And yet, reasonable Reader, see how wrong those men were, and grasp, if you can, the logic of the argument I'm about to set forth to you.

Is there anything more natural and more just than to put an end to it all, aided by someone who inadvertently treads on your toes, or drops some rather pointed remark in a moment of irritation occasioned by your thoughtlessness, or, indeed, has the misfortune to seem attractive to your mistress?

You go to some meadow and there, as did Nicole with the Bourgeois Gentilhomme, you try to make a quart when he parries with a tierce;[2] and so that the vengeance will be sure and complete, you present yourself to him with your chest bared, and you run the risk of getting yourself killed by your enemy so as to be avenged on him. – Obviously, nothing could be more logical, and yet you come across people who disapprove of this praiseworthy custom! But what is just as logical as all the rest is the fact that these same people who disapprove of it, and want it to be regarded as a grave crime, would treat anyone who refused to commit it even worse. More than one unhappy man has lost his reputation and his job so as to conform to their opinion; the result is that when you have the misfortune of having what is called *an affair of honour* on your hands, it wouldn't be a bad idea to draw lots to find out if you must conclude it in accordance with law or with custom, and since law and custom contradict each other, the judges could also play dice to decide on their verdict. – And it is probably to a decision of this kind that we need to resort in order to explain how and why my journey lasted exactly forty-two days.

4

My room is situated on the forty-fifth degree of latitude, according to the measurement of Fr Beccaria[3]; it stretches from east to west; it forms a long rectangle, thirty-six paces in circumference if you hug the wall. My journey will, however, measure much more than this, as I will be crossing it frequently lengthwise, or else diagonally, without any rule or method. – I will even follow a zigzag path, and I will trace out every possible geometrical trajectory if need be. I don't like people who have their itineraries and ideas so clearly sorted out that they say, 'Today I'll make three visits, I'll write four letters, and I'll finish that book I started.' – My soul is so open to every kind of idea, taste and sentiment; it so avidly receives everything that presents itself!... – And why would it turn down the pleasures that are scattered along life's difficult path? They are so few and far between, so thin on the ground, that you'd need to be mad not to stop, and even turn away from your path, and pick up all of those that lie within reach. There's no more attractive pleasure, in my view, than following one's ideas wherever they lead, as the hunter pursues his game, without even trying to keep to any set route. And so, when I travel through my room, I rarely follow a straight line: I go from my table towards a picture hanging in a corner; from there I set out obliquely towards the door; but even though, when I begin, it really is my intention to go there, if I happen to meet my armchair en route, I don't think twice about it, and settle down in it without further ado. – It's an excellent piece of furniture, an armchair; above all, it's highly useful for any man inclined to meditation. During the long winter evenings, it is sometimes sweet and sometimes sensible to spread out in it at your ease, far from the din of crowded assemblies. – A nice fire, books, pens; how many resources there are against boredom! And what a pleasure it is, too, to forget your books and your pens and instead poke your fire, succumbing to a gentle contemplation, or arranging a few rhymes to amuse your friends! Then the hours slip away over you, and silently fall into eternity, without making you feel their melancholy passage.

5

Once you've left my armchair, walking towards the north, you come into view of my bed, which is placed at the far end of my room: it's a most agreeable sight. It is situated in the most pleasant spot imaginable: the first rays of the sun come to disport themselves on my bed curtains. – I can see them, on fine summer days, advancing along the white wall as the sun slowly rises: the elm trees outside my window break up these rays in a thousand different ways, and make them sway on my pink and white bed, which sheds the charming hue of their reflections on every side. – I can hear the indistinct twittering of the swallows who have taken over the roof of the house and the other birds who live in the elms: then, a thousand cheerful ideas fill my mind; and nobody in the whole world wakes up in such a pleasant and peaceful way as I do.

I must confess that I love to bask in these sweet moments, and that I always prolong as much as I possibly can the pleasure of meditating in the snug warmth of my bed. – Is there any theatre which arouses the imagination more, or awakens more tender ideas, than this piece of furniture in which I sometimes lose myself? – Modest Reader, don't be alarmed; – but couldn't I be describing the happiness of a lover embracing for the first time a virtuous wife in his arms? An ineffable pleasure, which my evil destiny condemns me never to enjoy! Isn't it in a bed that a mother, overwhelmed with euphoria at the birth of her son, forgets the pains she has suffered? It is here that fantastic pleasures, the fruit of imagination and hope, come to arouse us. – Finally, it is here, in our delightful beds, that we can forget, for one half of our life, the sorrows of the other half. But what a host of thoughts both agreeable and melancholy come thronging into my brain all at once! An amazing mixture of terrible and delightful situations!

A bed witnesses our birth and death; it is the unvarying theatre in which the human race acts out, successively, its captivating dramas, laughable farces, and dreadful tragedies. – It is a cradle bedecked with flowers; – it is the throne of love; – it is a sepulchre.

6

This chapter is meant for metaphysicians, and for them alone. It will shed the greatest light on the nature of man: it is the prism which will make it possible to analyse and break down the faculties of man, separating out his animal vitality from the pure rays of the intelligence.

It would be impossible for me to explain how and why I burnt my fingers when I took my first steps at the start of my journey, unless I explained to the reader, in the greatest detail, my system *of the soul and the beast*. – This metaphysical discovery has indeed such a profound influence on my ideas and my actions that it would be extremely difficult to understand this book if I did not give you the key right at the start.

I have come to the conclusion, by way of various observations, that man is composed of a soul and a beast. – These two beings are absolutely distinct, but so closely fitted together, or one on top of the other, that the soul must have a certain superiority over the beast to be in a position to draw a distinction between them.

I hold it on the authority of an old teacher (as far back as I can remember) that Plato called matter *the other*. All well and good; but I would prefer to give this name first and foremost to the beast that is joined to our souls. It is really this substance that is the other, and which teases and torments us in so strange a fashion. Everyone is more or less aware that man is double; but the reason – they say – is that he is composed of a soul and a body; and they accuse this body of I don't know how many things, but quite irrelevantly, I can assure you, since it is just as incapable of feeling as it is of thinking. It is the beast that is behind it all – that sensitive creature, perfectly distinct from the soul, a real *individual*, which has its separate existence, its tastes, its inclinations, its will, and which is higher than the other animals only because it is better brought up and endowed with more perfect organs.

Ladies and gentlemen, be as proud of your intelligence as you want; but beware of the *other*, especially when the two of you get together!

I have experienced I don't know how many times the union of these two heterogeneous creatures. For example, I have clearly realised that the soul can make the beast obey it, and, contrariwise, the beast often forces the soul to act against its inclination. In the rule book, the one has the legislative power, and the other the executive power; but these two powers often clash. – The great art of a man of genius lies in being fully able to train his beast so that it can get along by itself, whereupon the soul, delivered from this painful contact, can rise up to heaven.

But we need to make this clear with an example.

When you read a book, sir, and a more agreeable idea suddenly strikes on your imagination, your soul straight away pounces on it and forgets the book, while your eyes mechanically follow the words and the lines; you come to the end of the page without understanding it, and without remembering what you have read. – This comes from the fact that your soul, having ordered its companion to read to it, did not warn it of the brief absence on which it was about to embark; as a result, *the other* continued to read even though your soul was no longer listening.

7

Doesn't that seem clear enough to you? Here's another example:

One day last summer, I was making my way on foot to Court. I had spent the whole morning painting, and my soul, enjoying its meditations on painting, left it to the beast to transport me to the King's palace.

'What a sublime art is painting!' my soul was thinking; 'happy is the man who has been touched by the spectacle of nature, who is not obliged to paint pictures for a living, and who does not paint merely as a pastime, but is struck by the majesty of a beautiful physiognomy and the admirable play of the light that suffuses the human face with a thousand subtle hues! He attempts to approach in his works the sublime effects of nature. Happy, too, is the painter whom the love of landscape leads out on solitary excursions, who is able to express on canvas the feeling of melancholy inspired in him by a gloomy wood or a deserted countryside! His productions imitate and reproduce nature; he creates new seas and dark caves on which the sun has never shone: at his order, green copses emerge from nothingness, and the blue of the sky is reflected in his pictures; he knows the art of fanning the breezes and making the tempests roar. At other times, he offers to the eye of the bewitched spectator the delightful landscapes of ancient Sicily: you can see panic-stricken nymphs taking flight through the reeds from some satyr in hot pursuit; temples of majestic build raise their proud heads above the sacred forest that encloses them: the imagination loses itself along the silent roads of this ideal country; the blue horizons merge gently into the sky, and the whole landscape, mirrored in the waters of a tranquil river, forms a spectacle that no lagoon can describe.'

As my soul was reflecting thus, *the other* kept right on going – God knows where! – Instead of making its way to Court, as it had been ordered to, it drifted away so far leftwards that, by the time my soul caught up with it, it was already at the door of Mme de Hautcastel, half a mile away from the royal palace.

I will leave it to the reader to imagine what would have happened if *the other* had entered all by itself the home of such a beautiful lady.

8

While it's a useful and pleasant thing to have a soul that is so independent of matter that it can send matter off on its travels all by itself when this seems a good idea, this faculty also has its disadvantages. To it, for instance, I owe the burn that I mentioned in a previous chapter. – I usually entrust my beast with the task of preparing my breakfast; it is my beast which toasts the bread for me and cuts it into slices. It makes a lovely cup of coffee, and very often drinks it all by itself without my soul being in the least involved, unless the latter enjoys watching the beast work. However, this is rare and difficult to bring about since it's easy, while carrying out some mechanical operation, to think of something else entirely; but it's extremely difficult to watch yourself acting, so to speak. Or rather, to explain it in terms of my system, it's difficult to give your soul the task of examining the doings of the beast, and to watch it at work without joining in. – This is the most astonishing metaphysical tour de force that man can perform.

I'd laid my fire tongs on the embers to toast my bread; and a short while afterwards, while my soul was off on its travels, a burning log suddenly rolled out onto the hearth: – my poor beast held out its hand to take the tongs, and I burnt my fingers.

9

I hope I've set out my ideas in enough detail in the previous chapters to give the reader something to think about, and to put him in a position where he can make his own brilliant discoveries in this area: he will not fail to be pleased with himself, if one day he manages to send his soul off on its travels all by itself; the pleasures that this faculty will afford him will outweigh the misunderstandings that may result. Is there any more deeply satisfying pleasure than that of spreading out one's existence in this way, occupying heaven and earth at once, and thereby doubling, so to speak, one's being? – Is it not the eternal, never-fulfilled desire of man to increase his powers and his faculties, to want to be where he is not, to recall the past and to live in the future? – He wishes to command armies and preside over academies; he wants to be adored by beautiful women and, if he possesses all these things, he then longs for tranquillity, for country fields, and he starts to envy the shepherd's little hut: his plans and his hopes continually founder on the real misfortunes that are an integral part of human nature; he cannot find happiness. A quarter of an hour travelling with me will show him the way to it.

Ah, why didn't he leave it to *the other* to take care of those wretched tasks and that ambition which torments him? – Come, you poor wretch! Make an effort to break out of your prison, and, from the heights of heaven to which I will lead you, from the midst of the celestial orbs and the empyrean – look at the beast, launched out into the world, chasing after fortune and honours all by itself; see the gravity with which it walks among men; the crowd parts respectfully to let it through, and, believe you me, nobody will realise that it is all alone; the throng amidst which it walks is not in the least concerned whether or not it has a soul, whether or not it thinks. – A thousand sentimental women will fall head over heels in love with your beast, and not even realise the fact; your beast may even rise, without any help from your soul, to the highest favour and the greatest fortune. – Finally, I wouldn't be the least bit surprised if, on our return from the empyrean, your soul found itself within the beast of a great lord.

10

Don't get the idea that, instead of keeping my word and giving a description of my journey around my room, I'm merely beating about the bush and evading the issue; you'd be quite wrong. No, my journey is really and truly continuing; and while my soul, withdrawing into itself, was in the last chapter exploring the tangled and twisted paths of metaphysics, *I* was in my armchair, in which I had leant back so that its two front legs were raised two inches above the ground; and by leaning to the right and the left, and thereby advancing slowly forward, I had imperceptibly come right up to the wall. – This is the way I travel when I'm not in any hurry. – Here my hand had mechanically taken down the portrait of Mme de Hautcastel, and *the other* was diverting itself by brushing off the dust with which the portrait was covered. – This occupation gave it a tranquil pleasure, and this pleasure communicated itself to my soul, even though the latter was lost in the vast plains of the sky. It's worth observing in this respect that, when the spirit travels thus through space, it is still attached to the senses by some secret link; as a result, without being distracted from its occupations, it can participate in the joys and pleasures of *the other*; but if this pleasure increases to a certain degree, or if it is struck by some unexpected sight, the soul immediately reassumes its place as quick as a flash of lightning.

This is just what happened to me as I was cleaning the portrait.

As the cloth wiped the dust away and revealed curls of blonde hair, and the garland of roses that crowns them, my soul, although far away in the sun to which it had transported itself, felt a slight quiver in its heart, and empathetically shared my pleasure. This pleasure became less indistinct and more intense when the cloth, in one single sweep, laid bare the gleaming forehead of that enchanting physiognomy; my soul was on the point of leaving the heavens to come and enjoy the spectacle. But if my soul had been at the Champs-Elysées, or attending a concert of cherubs, it wouldn't have stayed there for even half a second when its companion, taking an increasing interest in its work, decided to seize a wet sponge that was handed to it and immediately proceeded to draw it over the eyebrows and the eyes – over the nose –

over the cheeks – over that mouth; – ah, God! How my heart beats! – over the chin, over the breast: it took no more than a minute; the whole face seemed to be reborn and to emerge from nothingness. – My soul came sweeping down from heaven like a falling star; it found *the other* in a state of enraptured ecstasy, and succeeded in increasing its bliss by sharing it. This strange and unforeseen situation made time and space disappear for me. – I existed at a moment in the past, and I grew young again, against the order of nature. – Yes, here she is, that adored woman, it really is her, I can see her smiling; she's going to speak, she's going to tell me she loves me. – What a gaze! come, let me press you to my heart, soul of my life, my second existence! – come and share my exaltation and my happiness! – This moment was brief, but it was ravishing: frigid Reason soon regained control, and in the space of the twinkling of an eye, I grew a whole year older: – my heart became cold and frozen, and I found myself on the same level as the throng of indifferent people who weigh down the globe.

11

We mustn't run ahead of ourselves: my haste to communicate to the reader my system of the soul and the beast has made me abandon the description of my bed sooner than I should have done; when I've finished it, I'll carry on with my journey from the place where I left off in the last chapter. – I would merely ask you to remember once again that we have left *my other half* holding the portrait of Mme de Hautcastel, right next to the wall, four steps away from my desk. I had forgotten, as I was talking about my bed, to advise any man who can do so to have a pink and white bed: it is certain that colours influence us so much that they can brighten or sadden our mood with their nuances. – Pink and white are two colours dedicated to pleasure and happiness. – Nature, in giving these colours to the rose, has given to the rose the crown of Flora's empire; and when the heavens wish to announce to the world that a fine day lies ahead, they tint the clouds with this charming hue at sunrise.

One day we were struggling up a short cut: dear Rosalie was in front; her agility gave her wings: we could not keep up with her. – Suddenly, having reached the summit of a mound, she turned back to us to catch her breath, and smiled at our slowness. – Never, perhaps, had the two colours whose praises I am singing scored such a triumph. – Her flaming cheeks, her coral lips, her gleaming teeth, her alabaster neck, set against a background of verdure, struck every eye. We just had to stop to gaze at her: I won't say anything about her blue eyes, nor of the gaze she directed at us then, since it would take me away from my subject, and in any case I think about it as little as I possibly can. I need merely to have given the finest possible example of the superiority of these two colours over all others, and of their influence on the happiness of men.

I won't go any further today. What subject could I discuss that would not be insipid? What idea is not effaced by *that* idea? – I don't even know when I'll be able to carry on with my work. – If I do continue it, and the reader wants to see how it ends, let him address his request to the angel who distributes our thoughts, and ask him not to confuse the image of that mound with the throng of disjointed thoughts that he keeps throwing at me.

Without this precaution, it's all over as far as my journey is concerned.

12

....
....
.... the
mound ....
....
....
....
....

13

All efforts are in vain; I'll have to defer everything to a later date and stay put where I am: it's a military staging post.

14

I said that I am singularly fond of meditating in the snug warmth of my bed, and that its agreeable colour contributes greatly to the pleasure I derive from it.

In order to procure me this pleasure, my servant has been given orders to come into my room half an hour before the time I have decided to get up. I can hear him walking softly about and discreetly *fiddling with things* in my room, and this noise gives me the gratification of being aware of myself as I doze: a delicate pleasure, quite unknown to many people.

You are awake just enough to realise that you are not *entirely* awake, and to calculate, confusedly, that the hour for business and other vexations is still in the hourglass of time. Imperceptibly, my man starts to make more noise; it's so difficult to avoid doing so! In any case, he knows that the fateful hour is drawing nigh. – He looks at my watch, and makes the pendants on its chain jingle to warn me; but I turn a deaf ear; and so as to prolong even more this delightful hour, there isn't a single delaying tactic I won't inflict on that poor wretch. I have a hundred preliminary orders to give him in order to gain some extra time. He knows perfectly well that my orders, which I give him rather gruffly, are merely excuses for my staying in bed without apparently wishing to do so. He pretends not to notice, and I'm really very grateful to him for that.

Finally, once I have exhausted all my resources, he advances into the middle of the room and stands right there, his arms folded, perfectly motionless.

As you will concede, it wouldn't be possible to disapprove of my thoughts with more spirit and discretion: so I never resist this tacit invitation; I hold out my arms to show that I have understood, and there I am, sitting down.

If the reader will reflect on my servant's behaviour, he'll be able to convince himself that, in certain delicate matters such as this, simplicity and common sense are worth infinitely more than the greatest astuteness of mind. I dare say that the most studied speech about the drawbacks of the spoken word would not force me to leave my bed as promptly as does the mute reproach of M. Joannetti.

This M. Joannetti is a thoroughly decent chap, and at the same time he is of all men the one who best suits a traveller such as myself. He is used to the frequent journeys of my soul, and he never laughs at the fecklessness of *the other*; he even directs her, sometimes, when she's alone, so that you might say that she is then governed by two souls; when she gets dressed, for instance, he gives me a signal to warn me that she's about to put on her stockings inside out, or her coat before her jacket. – My soul has often enjoyed watching poor Joannetti running after that crazy beast under the vaults of the citadel to tell her that she'd forgotten her hat; – or, on another occasion, her handkerchief.

One day (dare I confess it?), without this faithful servant who caught up with her at the foot of the stairs, the muddle-head would have gone off to Court without a sword, as boldly as the grand master of ceremonies carrying his august staff.

15

'I say, Joannetti,' I told him, 'hang this portrait back in its place.' – He had helped me to clean it, and hadn't any more inkling of what had produced my chapter on the portrait than of what happens in the moon. He it was who, of his own volition, had presented the wet sponge to me, and by this apparently insignificant gesture had made my soul sweep across a hundred million leagues in a single instant. Instead of putting it back in its place, he kept hold of it and wiped it in his turn. – A difficulty, a problem that needed solving, made him look inquisitive – as I noticed.

'Well,' I said to him, 'what's the problem with this portrait?'

'Oh! Nothing, sir.'

'But what's the matter, then?'

He placed it on one of the appointment books on my desk; then, taking a few steps back from it, he said, 'I would like sir to explain why this portrait always looks at me, wherever I happen to be in the room. In the morning, when I'm making the bed, its face turns towards me, and if I go to the window, it still watches me and follows me with its eyes while I move about.'

'With the result, dear Joannetti,' said I, 'that if the room were full of people, this lovely lady would turn every which way and eye up everyone at once?'

'Oh, yes, sir!'

'She would smile at all those coming and going, just as she does at me?'

Joannetti didn't reply. – I spread out in my armchair and, lowering my head, I abandoned myself to the most serious meditations. – What a flash of insight! Poor lover! While you are kicking your heels far from your mistress, who has perhaps already found a replacement for you, while you are avidly fixing your eyes on her portrait and imagining (at least when it comes to the painting) that you are the only one being gazed at, the perfidious effigy, just as unfaithful as the original, gazes at everything around her, and smiles at everyone.

Here we have a moral resemblance between certain portraits and their models, which no philosopher, no painter and no observer had yet noticed.

I am making discovery after discovery!

16

Joannetti was still standing there awaiting the explanation he had asked me for. I poked my head out of the folds of my *travelling coat*, into which I had withdrawn to meditate at my ease and to recover from the gloomy reflections I had just been making.

'Don't you see, Joannetti,' I told him after a moment of silence, turning my armchair to face him, 'don't you see that since a painting is a plane surface, the light rays that leave each part of that surface?...'

Joannetti, on hearing this explanation, opened his eyes so wide that he showed their whites; on top of that, his mouth was hanging half open: these two movements in the human face announce, according to the celebrated Le Brun[4], that astonishment has reached its acme. It was my beast, no doubt, that had embarked on this long speech; my soul knew, in any case, that Joannetti was completely ignorant of what a plane surface is, and even more of what light rays are: the prodigious dilation of his pupils had made me withdraw into myself again, so that I plunged my head down into the collar of my travelling coat so very deeply that I managed to hide it almost completely.

I decided to have lunch in this spot: the morning was well advanced, and if I'd taken one step more in my room, I wouldn't have eaten until the evening. I slipped to the edge of my armchair and, resting my two feet on the mantelpiece, patiently awaited my meal. – This is a delightful posture to adopt; it would, I believe, be difficult to find another which combines so many advantages, and is as comfortable on the inevitable breaks that occur during a long journey.

Rosine, my faithful bitch, never fails at such times to come and tug at my coat-tails so I'll take her onto my lap; here she finds a bed all ready for her, nice and snug, at the summit of the angle formed by the two parts of my body: a consonantal V gives you a splendid image of my posture. Rosine leaps up onto me, and I never pick her up as quickly as she would like. I often just find her there, without any idea of how she got there. My hands spontaneously arrange themselves in the way most favourable to her well-being, either because there is a certain empathy between this lovable beast and myself, or merely by chance; – but I don't believe in chance, that gloomy system – that word which signifies nothing. – I'd rather believe in magnetism; – I'd rather believe in Martinism[5]. – No, I'll never believe in it.

There is such a reality in the relations that exist between these two animals that, when I place my two feet on the mantelpiece, out of mere absent-mindedness, when dinner-time is still a while away and I haven't the slightest intention of *stopping off*, nonetheless, Rosine, alert to this movement, betrays the pleasure she feels by gently wagging her tail; discretion keeps her in her place, and *the other*, who notices this, is grateful to her: although they are incapable of reasoning on the cause that produces it, a mute dialogue starts up between them, a very pleasant sensation of being linked together, and one that absolutely cannot be attributed to chance.

17

Don't let anyone start telling me off for being prolix in my details: all travellers behave the same way. When anyone sets off to climb Mont Blanc, or goes to visit the wide-open tomb of Empedocles,[6] he never fails to describe the smallest details precisely: the number of people, the number of mules, the quality of the provisions, the excellent appetite of the travellers... Everything, in short, up to and including the times his mounts stumble, is painstakingly recorded in his diary, for the instruction of the sedentary world. On this principle, I have decided to talk about my dear Rosine, that dear animal that I love with real affection, and to devote an entire chapter to her.

Over the six years we have been living together, there hasn't been the slightest cooling off in our feelings for one another; or, if a few little altercations *have* arisen between myself and her, I admit in all good faith that the greatest wrong was always on my side, and that Rosine has always taken the first steps towards reconciliation.

In the evenings, whenever she's been scolded, she goes off sadly, without a murmur; the next day, at daybreak, she's beside my bed, in an attitude of great respect; and at the least movement from her master, at the least sign that he is awakening, she announces her presence by banging her tail rapidly and repeatedly on my night table.

And why would I refuse my love to this affectionate being, who has never ceased to love me ever since we started to live together? My memory isn't good enough to be able to draw up a list of all the people who have taken an interest in me and then forgotten me. I've had a few friends, several mistresses, a host of love affairs, even more acquaintances; – and now I don't mean a thing to any of those people, who have even forgotten my name.

How many protestations of affection they uttered, how many favours they offered! I could always count on their fortunes – they said – on an eternal friendship, without reservation!

My dear Rosine, who has never offered me any favours, in fact does me the greatest favour that can be shown to humanity: she loved me once, and she still loves me today. So I can say quite without fear that I love her with a portion of the same sentiment that I bestow on my friends.

You can say what you like about it.

18

We left Joannetti standing motionless and astonished in front of me, waiting for the end of the sublime explanation that I had started.

When he saw me suddenly withdraw my head into my dressing gown, and thus bring my explanation to an end, he didn't for a moment doubt that I must have had good reasons for stopping short, and he deduced that he must have completely stumped me with the difficulty of his question.

Despite the superiority he thereby acquired over me, he did not feel the slightest impulse of pride, and did not seek to drive his advantage home. – After a short moment of silence, he took the portrait, set it back in its place and quietly withdrew, on tiptoe. – He clearly sensed that his presence was a kind of humiliation for me, and his delicacy bade him withdraw without letting me see. – I felt a warm appreciation for his behaviour on this occasion, which gave him an even more prominent position in my heart. He will doubtless have a place in the reader's heart too; and if there is anyone so insensitive as to refuse *that* to him after reading the following chapter, then Heaven has doubtless given him a heart of stone.

19

'Dammit!' I said to him one day, 'that's the third time I've ordered you to fetch me a brush! You dunderheaded brute!' He didn't say a word in reply: the day before, he hadn't said a word in reply to a similar outburst from me, either. 'But he's so punctilious!' I kept thinking; I just couldn't understand it.

'Go and get a cloth to clean my shoes,' I said angrily. As he went off, I felt sorry for having been so brusque with him. My wrath vanished completely when I saw the care he was taking to clean the dust away from my shoes without touching my stockings: I laid my hand on him in a sign of reconciliation.

'So,' I said to myself, 'there are men who clean the muck off others' shoes for money?' This word, *money*, was a flash of light that illumined my mind. I suddenly remembered that it had been a long time since I'd given any money to my servant.

'Joannetti,' I said to him, pulling my foot away, 'do you have any money?' A half-smile of justification appeared on his lips at this question.

'No, sir; for the past week I haven't had a penny to my name; I've spent everything that belonged to me on your little errands.'

'And what about the brush? You spent your money on that, I imagine?'

He smiled again. He could have said to his master, 'No, I'm not an empty-headed *brute*, as you had the cruelty to call your faithful servant. Pay me the twenty-three pounds, ten pence and four farthings that you owe me, and I'll buy your brush for you.' He let himself be mistreated unjustly rather than making his master feel obliged to blush in shame over his own wrath.

May Heaven bless him! Philosophers! Christians! Have you noted this? 'Look here, Joannetti,' I said, 'look here, just go and buy the brush.'

'But sir, do you want to be left just like that, with one shoe white and the other black?'

'Go on, I tell you, go and buy the brush; you can just leave that dust on my shoe.'

He went out; I picked up the cloth and spent a delightful while cleaning my left shoe, on which I let fall a tear of repentance.

20

The walls of my room are decorated with engravings and paintings that make it singularly attractive. I wish with all my heart I could let the reader examine them one after the other, to amuse him and distract him in the course of the long journey we still have to make if we are ever to reach my desk; but it's just as impossible to explain a picture clearly as it is to draw an accurate portrait on the basis of a description.

What emotion would he not feel, for instance, when he contemplated the first engraving that offers itself to his gaze? – In it he would see the unhappy Charlotte, wiping with a slow and trembling hand Albert's pistols.[7] – Dark presentiments, and all the anguish of hopeless and inconsolable love are imprinted on her features, while the cold-hearted Albert, surrounded by bags full of judicial reports and old papers of every kind, turns coldly round to wish his friend a safe journey. How many times have I not been tempted to break the glass over this engraving, to pull that Albert away from his table, tear him limb from limb, and trample him underfoot! But there will always be too many Alberts in this world. Which sensitive man does not have his Albert, with whom he is obliged to live, and against whom the outpourings of his soul, the sweet emotions of his heart, and the impulses of his imagination break like the waves against the rocks? Happy the man who finds a friend whose heart and mind harmonise with his; a friend united to him by a conformity of tastes, feelings and interests; a friend who is not tormented by ambition or egotism; – one who prefers the shade of a tree to the pomp and circumstance of a court! – Happy the man who possesses a friend!

21

I had one once: death has taken him away from me; it seized him at the very start of his career, just as his friendship had become an urgent need for my heart. – We supported each other in the harsh travails of war; we shared one pipe between the two of us; we drank out of the same cup; we slept under the same canvas, and, given the unhappy circumstances we found ourselves in, the place where we lived together was for us a new fatherland: I have seen him encountering all the perils of war, and a catastrophic war at that. – Death seemed to spare each of us for the sake of the other: it fired off all its darts at him, a thousand times over, without hitting him: but as a result I merely felt his loss all the more keenly. The tumult of arms, and the impetuosity that grips the soul at the sight of danger, would perhaps have prevented his cries from reaching my heart. – His death would have been useful to his country and fateful to his enemies: – I would have regretted it less. – But to lose him in the enchanting surroundings of winter quarters! To see him expire in my arms just as he seemed to be the very picture of health, just as our friendship was growing even closer in this atmosphere of repose and tranquillity! – Ah, I'll never get over his loss! And yet his memory now lives only in my heart; it no longer exists among those who surrounded him and who have replaced him; this idea makes the feeling of his loss even more painful for me. Nature, likewise indifferent to the fate of individuals, puts on her dazzling spring dress and decks herself out in all her beauty around the cemetery where he rests. The trees are covered with leaves and intertwine their branches; the birds sing in the foliage; the flies buzz among the flowers; everything breathes joy and life in this dwelling place of the dead: – and in the evenings, whilst the moon shines in the sky, and I meditate near this sad spot, I can hear the cricket gaily pursuing its indefatigable song, hidden away in the grass that covers my friend's silent tomb. The imperceptible destruction of creatures and all the woes of humankind count as nothing in the great universe. – The death of a sensitive man who expires in the midst of his heartbroken friends, and that of a butterfly killed off by the chill morning air in the calyx of a flower, mark two similar epochs in the course of nature. Man is nothing but a phantom, a shadow, a vapour that vanishes into thin air…

But the dawn starts to lighten up the morning sky; the dark ideas that had been troubling me so greatly evaporate with the night, and hope is born again in my heart. – No, he who thus floods the east with light did not make it gleam on my eyes merely to plunge me quickly into the night of non-being. He who laid out this immeasurable horizon, he who raised up these enormous masses, he whose sun sheds a golden glow on the icy mountain summits, is also he who ordered my heart to beat and my mind to think.

No, my friend has not entered non-being; whatever the barrier that separates me from him, I will see him again. – It is not on a syllogism that I found my hope. – The flight of an insect through the air is enough to persuade me; and often the sight of the countryside, the perfume in the air, and a certain mysterious charm shed all around me, so elevate my thoughts that an invincible proof of immortality forces its way into my heart and occupies it wholly.

22

For a long time, the chapter I have just written was at the tip of my pen, but I kept rejecting it. I had promised myself that in this book I would display only the cheerful aspect of my soul; but this plan slipped out of my hands, like so many others: I hope that the sensitive reader will forgive me for having asked a few tears of him; and if anyone finds that *in all truth* I should have cut this chapter, he can tear it out of his copy, or even throw the book on the fire.

It's enough that your heart finds it to your liking, my dear Jenny, you, the best and most beloved of women: – you, the best and most beloved of sisters; it is to you that I dedicate my work; if it meets with your approval, it will also meet with that of all sensitive and delicate hearts; and if you will pardon the foolish remarks that I sometimes let drop, I will defy all the censors in the world.

23

I will only say a word or two about the next engraving.

It represents the family of the unfortunate Ugolino[8] dying of starvation: around him, one of his sons lies motionless at his feet; the others hold out their enfeebled arms to him and beg him for bread, while the wretched father, leaning against a pillar in the prison, his eyes wild and staring, his face frozen in the horrible tranquillity that comes with the last vicissitudes of despair, simultaneously dies his own death and that of all his children, and suffers everything that human nature can suffer.

Brave Chevalier d'Assas, behold how you expire under a thousand bayonets, making one last courageous effort and showing a heroism that, these days, we no longer witness![9]

And you who weep under those palm trees, unhappy Negro woman! You whom a barbarian, who of course was not an Englishman, betrayed and abandoned… ah, more than that! He had the cruelty to sell you like a vile slave, despite your love and the services you had rendered him, despite the fruit of his tender affection that you bear within your womb, – I will not pass in front of your image without paying you the homage that is owed to your sensitive nature and your tribulations!

Let us pause awhile before this other picture: it is a young shepherdess who is tending her flock all alone on the summit of the Alps: she is sitting on an old pine trunk that the winters have overthrown and turned white; her feet are covered by the broad leaves of a clump of *cacalia*, from which a lilac flower rises over her head.[10] Lavender, thyme, anemones, centauries, flowers of every species that we find difficult to grow in our hothouses and our gardens, and that spring up in the Alps in all their original beauty, form the brilliant carpet over which her sheep wander. – Gentle shepherdess, tell me where one can find the happy corner of the earth that you inhabit! From what distant sheepfold did you set out this morning at sunrise? – Could I not go and live there with you? – But, alas! it will not be long before the mild tranquillity you enjoy evaporates; the demon of war, not content with making the cities desolate, will soon be bringing upheaval and terror right into your solitary retreat. Already the soldiers are marching up;

I can see them advancing from mountain to mountain, and coming ever closer to the skies. – The roar of the cannon can be heard in the lofty dwelling place of thunder. – Fly, shepherdess, urge on your flock, hide away in the wildest and remotest caverns: there is no rest on this melancholy earth.

24

I don't know how it has come about, but for some time all my chapters have been ending on a sinister note. In vain I fix my gaze on some pleasant object as I start to write them, – in vain I embark in calm weather: I soon run into a squall that drives me off course. – To put an end to this agitation, which leaves me no longer master of my ideas, and to assuage the beatings of my heart, which endearing images have agitated far too greatly, I can see no other remedy than a little bit of speechifying.

And this speech will be on painting; after all, there is no way of holding forth on any other topic. I cannot altogether come down from the heights to which I had risen just now: in any case, it's like the hobby horse of my Uncle Toby.[11]

I would like to say, in passing, a few words on the question of which of those two charming arts, painting and music, is pre-eminent: yes, I want to put something in the scales, be it no more than a grain of sand or an atom.

They say in the painter's favour that he leaves something behind him; his pictures survive him and eternise his memory.

The answer is that musical composers also leave operas and concertos behind them; – but music is in thrall to fashion, and painting isn't. – The pieces of music that moved our forebears strike today's amateurs as ridiculous, and they end up being inserted into comic operas, to give a laugh to the descendants of those whom they once made weep.

The paintings of Raphael will delight posterity just as they delighted our ancestors.

That's my grain of sand.

25

'But what does it matter to *me*,' said Mme de Hautcastel to me one day, 'whether the music of Cherubini or Cimarosa[12] differs from that of their predecessors? – What does it matter that old music makes me laugh, so long as the new music moves me so delightfully? Is it necessary to my happiness, then, that my pleasures should resemble those of my great-great-grandfather? Why are you telling me about painting – an art which is appreciated by a very small class of people – whereas music enchants everything which lives and breathes?'

I don't really know, right now, what one could reply to this observation, which I didn't expect when I began this chapter.

And if I *had* foreseen it, perhaps I wouldn't have embarked on this little speech. And don't let anyone take this as a musician's trick. – I am *not* a musician, upon my honour; – no, I am not, as heaven and all those who have heard me play the violin will witness.

But supposing the merit of the art is equal on both sides, we should not hasten to conclude that the merit of one artist equals that of another. – You see children playing the harpsichord like great maestros; but you have never seen a good painter who is only twelve years old. Painting requires, as well as taste and sentiment, a thinking head, which musicians can manage without. Every day you can see men without heads and without hearts drawing ravishing sounds from a violin or a harp.

You can train the human beast to play the harpsichord; and when it is trained by a good master, the soul can travel at perfect ease, while the fingers go on mechanically creating sounds with which the soul has nothing to do. – Conversely, it is impossible to paint even the simplest thing in the world unless the soul deploys all its faculties on the task.

If, however, anyone took it into his head to distinguish between the music of composition and the music of performance, I have to confess that I would be perplexed. Alas! If all speechifiers were in good faith, this is how they would all conclude. – When you start to investigate a question, you usually adopt a dogmatic tone since you have secretly already made up your mind, just as in reality I had made up my mind in favour of painting, in spite of my hypocritical impartiality; but discussion awakens objections, and everything ends up in doubt.

26

Now that I've calmed down, I'm going to try and speak without too much emotion about the two portraits that come after the painting of the *Shepherdess of the Alps*.

Raphael! Your portrait could only have been painted by yourself. What other man would have dared undertake it? – Your open, sensitive, spiritual face expresses your character and your genius.

To please your shade, I have placed next to you the portrait of your mistress, whom every man in every age will hold eternally responsible for the loss of those sublime works which your premature death deprived the arts of.

When I examine Raphael's portrait, I am filled with an almost religious respect for this great man who, in the flower of his age, had surpassed the whole of antiquity, and whose pictures induce admiration and despair in modern artists. – My soul, as it admires this painting, feels a wave of indignation at that Italian woman who preferred her love to her lover, and who extinguished, as she clutched him to her bosom, that heavenly spark, that divine genius.

Wretched girl! Didn't you know that Raphael had announced he would paint a picture even finer than the *Transfiguration*? – Were you unaware that you were holding in your arms nature's favourite, the father of inspired creation, a sublime genius, a god?

While my soul makes these observations, its *companion*, fixing an attentive eye on the ravishing face of this fateful beauty, feels quite ready to forgive her for Raphael's death.

In vain does my soul rebuke her companion for her extravagant indulgence: she simply turns a deaf ear. – There ensues between these two ladies, on these types of occasion, a strange dialogue which all too often finishes to the advantage of the *bad principle*: I will keep a sample in reserve for a later chapter.

27

The engravings and paintings I have just been discussing fade away and vanish the moment you turn to the next picture: the immortal works of Raphael, Correggio[13] and the whole School of Italy could not stand up to the comparison. So I always keep it until last, as the pièce de résistance, when I grant a few curious people the pleasure of travelling with me; and I can assure you that, ever since I have been showing this sublime painting to connoisseurs and to the ignorant, to people in society, to workers, to women and children, and even to animals, I've always seen the spectators, of whatever sort or condition, show – each after his or her manner – signs of pleasure and amazement: so faithfully is nature rendered on it!

Ah! what picture could anyone present to you, gentlemen; and what spectacle could one place beneath your eyes, ladies, more sure of meeting with your approval than the faithful representation of yourselves? The painting of which I speak is a mirror, and nobody has ever yet taken it into their heads to criticise it; it is, for all those who look into it, a perfect picture, one with which it is impossible to find fault.

Doubtless, everyone will agree that it should be reckoned as one of the marvels of the country through which I am strolling.

I will pass over in silence the pleasure felt by the scientist meditating on the strange phenomenon of light that represents all the objects of nature on this polished surface. The mirror presents to the sedentary traveller a thousand interesting reflections, a thousand observations that make it a useful and precious object.

You whom love has held or still holds in its thrall, learn that it is in front of a mirror that he sharpens his arrows and plots his cruelties; it is here that he practises his manoeuvres, studies his moves, and prepares himself for the war he is about to declare; it is here that he trains himself to make those lingering glances, those little flirtatious expressions, those knowing pouts, just as an actor trains himself by gazing at his reflection before presenting himself to the public. Always impartial and true, a mirror restores to the spectator's eyes a vision of the roses of youth and the wrinkles of age without denigrating or flattering anyone. – It alone always tells the truth to the great, unlike all their other counsellors.

This advantage had led me to long for someone to invent a moral mirror in which all men could see themselves with their vices and their virtues. I was even thinking of offering a prize so that some academy could encourage this invention, when mature reflection proved to me how useless it would be.

Alas! it is so rare that ugliness recognises itself and smashes the mirror! In vain do mirrors multiply around us, and reflect light and truth with geometrical precision: just as the rays are about to penetrate our eyes and depict us exactly as we are, self-regard slips its deceitful prism between ourselves and our image, and presents us with a divinity.

And of all the prisms that have ever existed, from the first which came from the hands of the immortal Newton, none has possessed a force of refraction as powerful, or produced colours as agreeable and vivid, as the prism of self-esteem.

Now, since common mirrors announce the truth in vain, and in them everyone is happy with his face; since they cannot show men their physical imperfections, what would be the use of my moral mirror? Few people would look into it, and nobody would recognise himself or herself in it – apart from philosophers. – I even rather doubt that *they* would.

Taking the mirror for what it is, I hope that nobody will criticise me for having placed it above all the pictures of the School of Italy. The ladies, who are incapable of bad taste, and whose decision should settle everything, usually glance first at this picture when they enter an apartment.

I have seen these ladies and even certain young gallants forgetting their lovers or their mistresses at the ball, as well as the dancing and all the pleasures of the festivities, to contemplate with a notable self-indulgence this enchanting picture – and even honour it with a glance, from time to time, in the middle of the most lively *contredanse*.

So who could dispute the rank I accord it among the masterpieces of the art of Apelles[14]?

28

I had finally come right up to my desk; indeed, if I'd stretched out my arm, I would already have been able to touch the corner closest to me, when I saw that I was about to destroy the fruit of all my labours, and lose my life. – I ought to pass over the accident that befell me, so as not to discourage travellers; but it's so difficult to tip out of the post-chaise I use that you will be forced to admit that someone needs to be thoroughly unlucky – as unlucky as I am – to run such a danger. I found myself stretched out on the ground, completely toppled and overturned; and it all happened so quickly, so unexpectedly, that I would have been tempted to cast doubt on my ill luck if a buzzing in my head and a violent pain in my left shoulder had not proved its authenticity all too clearly to me.

It was yet another nasty trick played by *my other half*. – Startled by the voice of a poor man who had suddenly started to beg for alms at my door, and by the barking of Rosine, my other half suddenly swung my chair around before my soul could have time to warn her that there wasn't a brick behind to support it; the move was so powerful and sudden that my post-chaise found itself quite outside its centre of gravity and fell back on top of me.

This, I must confess, is one of the occasions on which I have had most cause to complain of my soul; instead of being vexed at the absent-mindedness she had just demonstrated, and telling off her companion for her over-precipitate movement, she forgot herself so far as to share the most *animal* resentment, and to maltreat that poor innocent man with harsh words.

'You lazy so-and-so, go and do some work!' she told him (an execrable way of addressing him, invented by avaricious and cruel wealth!).

'Sir,' he said then, to placate me, 'I'm from Chambéry…'[15]

'So much the worse for you.'

'I'm Jacques; it was me that you saw in the countryside; I was the one leading the sheep to the fields…'

'And what have you come here for?' My soul was starting to repent of the brutality of my first words. – I even think that she had repented a moment before letting them slip out. It's like when you unexpectedly come to a ditch or a quagmire on your road: you can see it, but you don't have time to avoid it.

Rosine finally brought me back to common sense and repentance; she had recognised Jacques, who had often shared his bread with her, and demonstrated her memory and gratitude with her affectionate pawings.

During this time Joannetti had been gathering the remains of my meal, which were destined to form his; he unhesitatingly gave them to Jacques.

Poor Joannetti!

Thus it is that, on my journey, I continually take lessons in philosophy and humanity from my servant and my dog.

29

Before going any further, I want to put paid to a doubt which might have crossed my readers' minds.

I wouldn't for anything in the world want to be suspected of having embarked on this journey merely because I couldn't think of anything to do – forced to do so, as it were, by mere circumstance; I assure you here, and swear by all I hold dear, that I had planned to undertake it long before the event that made me lose my liberty for forty-two days. This enforced retreat was merely an opportunity to set out on my journey earlier.

I know that the unnecessary protestation I am here uttering will seem suspect to certain people; – but I also know that suspicious people won't read this book; – they have enough to do already at home and at the homes of their friends; they have plenty of other things to keep them busy; – and good people *will* believe me.

I admit, however, that I'd have preferred to embark on this journey some other time, and that I'd have chosen Lent rather than Carnival to execute it: however, philosophical reflections granted me by Heaven greatly helped me to put up with the privation of the pleasures that Turin offers in great numbers in these moments of noise and agitation. 'It is beyond all doubt,' I kept saying to myself, 'that the walls of my room are not as magnificently decorated as those of a ballroom; the silence of my *cabin* isn't as good as the pleasant noise of music and dancing; but among the brilliant personages that you meet at those parties, there are certainly some who are more bored than I am.'

And why would I bother to consider people who are in a more agreeable situation than mine, when the world is swarming with people who are more unhappy than me? – Instead of transporting myself in my imagination to that superb *casin*[16], where so many beauties are eclipsed by young Eugénie, if I wish to consider myself happy, I need only pause awhile on the roads that lead there. – A heap of unfortunate folk, lying half naked under the porches of those sumptuous apartments, seem on the point of expiring from cold and misery. – What a sight! I wish this page of my book could be known throughout the world; I would like it to be known that, in this city – where everything breathes opulence –

during the coldest winter nights, a host of wretches sleep out in the open, with only a boundary stone or the threshold of some palace on which to lay their heads.

Here you see a group of children huddling close together so as not to die of cold. – There, it's a woman, shivering and voiceless to complain. – The passers-by come and go, quite untouched by a sight to which they are used. – The noise of the carriages, the voice of intemperance, the ravishing sounds of music, sometimes mingle with the cries of these unfortunates and create a horrible dissonance.

30

Anyone tempted to utter a hasty judgement on the city after reading the previous chapter would be quite mistaken. I mentioned the poor people you find there, their pitiful cries, and the indifference of certain people towards them; but I did not mention the host of charitable men who sleep while the others are enjoying themselves, get up at daybreak and go off to give aid and comfort to misfortune, without witnesses and without ostentation. – No, I won't pass that over in silence; – I want to write it on the back of the page *that the whole world must read.*

Thus, having shared their fortune with their brothers, having poured balm into these hearts afflicted by pain, they go into the churches, while exhausted vice sleeps on an eiderdown, and there they offer their prayers to God and thank him for his benefits: the light of the solitary lamp in the temple is still struggling against that of the dawning day, and already they are prostrating themselves at the foot of the altars; – and the Eternal, angered at the harshness and avarice of men, holds back his thunderbolt that was poised to strike!

31

I wanted to say something about these unfortunate people during my journey, since the idea of their misery has often come along to distract me en route. Sometimes, struck by the difference between their situation and mine, I would suddenly halt my berlin, and my room would seem to me prodigiously embellished. What useless luxury! Six chairs, two tables, a desk, a mirror – what ostentation! My bed in particular, my pink and white bed, and my two mattresses, seemed to me to rival the magnificence and the soft ease of the monarchs of Asia. – These reflections rendered the pleasures that I had been forbidden indifferent to me: and as I went from one reflection to the next, my sudden philosophical frame of mind became so marked that I could have seen a ball in the room next door, and heard the sound of violins and clarinets, without shifting from my place; – I would have heard with my own two ears the melodious voice of Marchesini[17], that voice which has so often made me ecstatic – yes, I would have heard it without feeling at all stirred; – even more, I would have looked on the most beautiful woman in Turin without the slightest emotion – Eugénie herself, elegantly dressed from head to toe by the hands of Mlle Rapous[18]. – Actually, I'm not so sure of that.

32

But allow me to ask you, gentlemen, do you still enjoy yourselves as much as you used to at the ball and the theatre? – For my part, I confess, for some time now, all crowded gatherings have inspired me with a certain terror. – In them, I am assailed by a sinister dream. – In vain I do all I can to drive it away, but it keeps coming back, like the dream in *Athalie*.[19] – This is perhaps because the soul, today flooded with dark ideas and tragic images, finds causes of sadness everywhere – just as a corrupted stomach converts the healthiest foods into poisons. – Anyway, here is my dream: – When I am at one of those parties, amidst that host of amiable and friendly men dancing and singing, and shedding tears at the tragedies, and expressing nothing but joy, frankness and cordiality, I tell myself, 'If, into this polite assembly, there suddenly entered a white bear, a philosopher, a tiger, or some other animal of that species, which climbed into the orchestra, crying in a crazed voice: "Wretched humans! Listen to the truth that speaks to you through my mouth: you are oppressed and tyrannised; you are unhappy; you are bored. – Shake off this lethargy!

' "You, musicians, start by smashing those instruments over each other's heads; let everyone arm himself with a dagger; leave aside all thoughts of relaxation and party-going; climb up into the boxes and slaughter everyone; let the women, too, dip their timid hands in blood!

' "Leave! You are free! Tear down your king from his throne, and your god from his sanctuary!"

'Well,' I say to myself, 'how many of these charming men would obey the tiger? – How many, perhaps, were thinking of doing so even before he came in? Who knows? – Weren't they dancing in Paris five years ago?

'Joannetti, close the doors and the windows. – I don't want to see the light any more; let no man enter my room; – place my sabre within reach of my hand, – you leave, too, and appear no more before me!'

33

'No, no, stay, Joannetti; stay, poor boy; and you too, my Rosine; you, who guess at my pains and assuage them with your friendly pawings; come, my Rosine; come. – V consonant and stop.'

34

The fall of my post-chaise has done the reader the service of shortening my journey by a good dozen or so chapters, since as I picked myself up again I found myself opposite and right in front of my desk, and there was no longer time to make any reflections on the number of engravings and pictures that I still had to get through, and which might have lengthened my little excursions on painting.

So, leaving on the right the portraits of Raphael and his mistress, the Chevalier d'Assas and the *Shepherdess of the Alps*, and making our way along the left, on the window side, we come to my window: this is the first and most obvious object that presents itself to the traveller's gaze, if you follow the route I have just indicated.

It is topped by a few notebooks serving as a library; – the whole thing is crowned by a bust at the peak of the pyramid, and this is the object that contributes the most to the embellishment of the landscape.

Pulling open the first drawer on the right, you find a writing case, paper of every kind, pens already sharpened, and sealing wax. – All this would fill the most indolent man with the itch to write. – I am sure, my dear Jenny, that if you were by chance to open this drawer, you would reply to the letter that I wrote you last year. – In the corresponding drawer lie, in a disordered pile, materials for the interesting story of *The Prisoner of Pignerol*[20], which you will soon be reading, my friends.

Between these two drawers is a recess into which I pop letters as soon as I receive them: here you can find all those that I have received over the last ten years; the oldest ones are arranged, by date, in several packets: the new ones are put there any old how; I have kept several of them dating back to my earliest youth.

What a pleasure it is to see recorded in these letters the interesting situations of our young years, and to be transported back again to those happy times that we will never see again!

Ah, my heart is full! What an intense, melancholy pleasure it feels when my eyes run over the lines traced by someone who is no longer alive. Here is his handwriting, it was his heart that guided his hand, and this letter is all I have left of him!

When I put my hand into this cubbyhole, I rarely emerge from it for the rest of the day. Thus it is that the traveller rapidly traverses several provinces of Italy, making a few hasty and superficial observations, before settling in Rome for months at a time. – This is the richest vein of the mine that I am quarrying. What a change in my ideas and my feelings! What a difference in my friends! When I compare them as they were and as they are today, I see them in a mortal frenzy, busied with plans that touch them now no more. We regarded a particular event as a great misfortune; but the end of the letter is missing, and the event is completely forgotten: I cannot know what it was all about. – A thousand prejudices besieged us; the world and the people in it were quite unknown to us; but also, what warmth in our dealings; what a bond of intimacy! What boundless trust!

We were happy in our errors. – And now: – Ah! it's so different! We have had to read, like everyone else, in the human heart; – and truth, falling in our midst like a cannon shell, has destroyed for ever the enchanted palace of illusion.

35

I could perfectly well, if I so pleased, write a chapter on this dried rose here, if the subject were worth the trouble: it's a carnival flower from last year. I myself went to pluck it from the greenhouses of the Valentino[21], and in the evening, one hour before the ball, full of hope and in a state of agreeable turmoil, I went to present it to Mme de Hautcastel. She took it, – and placed it on her dressing table without looking at it (and without looking at me, either). – But how could she have paid any attention to me! She was busy looking at herself. Standing in front of a great mirror, with her hair dressed, she was putting the finishing touches to her finery: she was so very preoccupied, her attention was so totally absorbed by the ribbons, gauze and pompons of every kind laid in a heap in front of her that I did not get a single glance, not one sign, from her. – I resigned myself: I humbly held her pins ready for her, all arranged in my hand; but as her lacemaker's pillow was more within her reach, she would take them from the pillow, – and if I held out my hand, she would take them from my hand – it made no difference; – and in order to take them, she would simply feel for them without taking her eyes away from her mirror, for fear that she might lose sight of herself.

For a moment I held a second mirror behind her, so she could better judge how she looked; and as her face was repeated from one mirror to the other, I then saw a whole row of coquettish women, none of whom paid me any attention. All in all – dare I admit it? – we made a really sad picture, my rose and I.

I finally lost patience, and no longer able to repress the resentment that was devouring me, I set down the mirror I was holding, and swept out in high dudgeon, without saying goodbye.

'You're going?' she said to me, turning this way so as to see her figure in profile. I didn't answer; but I listened for a while at the door to see the effect that my sudden exit would produce.

'Don't you see,' she said to her chambermaid, after a moment's silence, 'that this camisole is much too wide for my figure, especially at the bottom, and that we need to make a pannier for it with pins?'

How and why this dried rose finds itself here, on a notebook on my desk, is something I am certainly not going to say, since I have already declared that a dry rose didn't deserve a whole chapter.

Note well, ladies, that I'm not making any reflection on the adventure of the dried rose. I am not saying that Mme de Hautcastel was right or wrong in preferring her toilet to me, nor that I had the right to be received in any other fashion.

I will refrain even more deliberately from deducing from this any general conclusions as to the reality, strength and durability of the affections of ladies for their men friends. – I will content myself with sending this chapter (since chapter it is) out into the world, together with the rest of the journey, without addressing it to anyone, and without recommending it to anyone.

I will merely add one piece of advice for you, gentlemen: just get it firmly into your heads that, on the day of a ball, your mistress no longer belongs to you.

When she starts to dress, a lover is no longer any more important than a husband, and the ball alone becomes her lover.

Everyone knows, too, what a lover gains by forcibly trying to ensure that he is loved; so bear your afflictions with patience and laughter. And don't have any illusions, sir: if they take pleasure in seeing you at the ball, it's not in your capacity as a lover; it's because you are part of the ball, and are thus, in consequence, a fraction of her new conquest; you are a *decimal part* of a lover: or, perhaps, it's because you dance well, and will make her shine: finally, the most flattering thing about the welcome she gives you is probably that she hopes, by declaring a man of merit such as yourself to be her lover, that she will arouse the jealousy of her female friends; if it weren't for this consideration, she wouldn't even look at you.

So that's all clear; you will have to resign yourself and wait until your role as husband is finished. – I know more than one man who wishes he could get off as lightly.

36

I promised a dialogue between my soul and *the other*; but there are certain chapters that slip away from me, or rather there are others which flow from my pen as if in spite of myself, and put all my plans out: they include the chapter on my library, which I will make as short as possible. – The forty-two days are coming to an end, and an equal space of time would not suffice to finish the description of the rich land through which I am so agreeably travelling.

So, my library is composed of novels, since I have to admit it – yes, novels, and a few choice poets.

As if my own troubles weren't enough, I also voluntarily share those of a thousand imaginary characters, and I feel them as vividly as my own: how many tears I have shed for that unhappy Clarissa and for the lover of Charlotte!

But if I also seek out feigned afflictions, I find, conversely, in this imaginary world, the virtue, the goodness, the disinterest that I have never yet found combined in the real world in which I live. – In it, I find a woman of the kind I yearn for: never in a bad mood, never flighty or flirtatious, never evasive: I won't even mention beauty – you can rely on my imagination: I make her so beautiful that there is no cause whatever for complaint. Then, closing the book, which no longer corresponds to my ideas, I take her by the hand, and we wander together through a landscape a thousand times more delightful than that of Eden. What painter could depict the enchanted landscape into which I have placed the divinity of my heart! And what poet could ever describe the vivid and varied sensations that I experience in these enchanted regions!

How often have I cursed that Cleveland[22], who at every moment keeps embarking on new misfortunes that he could avoid! I cannot stand that book with its long chain of calamities; but if I open it to pass the time, I have to devour it right through to the end.

How could anyone leave that poor man among the Abaquis[23]? What would become of him among those savages? I dare even less to abandon him in the excursion he undertakes in his bid to break out of his captivity.

Finally, I share his pains so intimately, I take such a strong interest in him and his unfortunate family, that the appearance of the fierce Ruintons[24] makes my hair stand on end: a cold sweat breaks out all over me when I read this passage, and my alarm is just as intense and real as if I myself were to be roasted and eaten by those villains.

When I have wept and made love enough, I seek out some other poet, and I again set out for another world.

37

From the expedition of the Argonauts to the Assembly of Notables,[25] from the lowest depths of hell to the last fixed star beyond the Milky Way, to the confines of the universe, to the gates of chaos – this is the vast terrain which I wander across in every direction at leisure; for I do not lack time any more than I lack space. It is here that I transport my existence, on the trail of Homer, Milton, Virgil, Ossian[26], etc.

All the events that occur between these two eras, all the countries, all the worlds and all the beings who have lived between these two limits – it is all mine, it all belongs to me just as much and just as legitimately as the vessels that entered the Piraeus belonged to a certain Athenian.

Most of all I love the poets who transport me back to the most distant antiquity: the death of the ambitious Agamemnon, the Furies of Orestes and the whole tragic tale of the Atreids, persecuted by heaven, inspire in me a terror that modern events would be quite unable to arouse.

Behold the fateful urn that contains the ashes of Orestes! Who would not shudder at the sight? Electra! Unhappy sister, take comfort: it is Orestes himself who is bringing the urn, and those ashes are the ashes of his enemies.

We can no longer find river-banks such as those of the Xanthus or the Scamander; – we can no longer see plains such as those of Hesperia or Arcadia. Where now are the isles of Lemnos or Crete? Where is the celebrated labyrinth? Where is the rock that the abandoned Ariadne watered with her tears? – We no longer see heroes like Theseus, even less like Hercules; the men and even the heroes of today are pygmies.

So when I want to enjoy some ardent scene, and revel in it with all the str ength of my imagination, I boldly hold tight to the folds of the floating robe of the sublime blind poet of Albion, as he hurls himself at the heavens, and dares to approach the throne of the Everlasting. – What muse managed to sustain him at that height, to which no man before him had dared to raise his eyes? – From the dazzling celestial forecourt on which the avaricious Mammon gazed with envious eyes, I pass with horror into the huge caverns of Satan's dwelling place; – I take part in the infernal council, I mingle with the crowd of the rebel spirits, and I listen to their speeches.

But here I must admit to a failing for which I have often reproached myself.

I cannot help taking a certain interest in this poor Satan (I mean Milton's Satan) from the moment he is flung out of heaven. While critical of the stubbornness of the rebel spirit, I confess that the firmness he shows in the excess of his misfortune, and the greatness of his courage, wring admiration from me in spite of myself. – Although I am not unaware of the miseries that sprang from the fateful enterprise that led him to force the gates of hell and come to disturb the domestic peace of our first parents, I cannot, however hard I try, wish for a moment to see him perishing en route in the hurly-burly of chaos. I even think I would be willing to give him a helping hand, if it were not that decency restrains me. I follow his every move, and I enjoy travelling with him as much as if I were in good company. However much I reflect that, after all, he is a devil, that he is on his way to ruin the human race, that he is a real democrat, not of Athens but of Paris – none of this can cure me of my bias towards him.

What a grandiose plan! And what boldness in its execution!

When the spacious and triple gates of hell suddenly opened wide before him, and the deep pit of nothingness and night appeared at his feet in all its horror, – he surveyed with an intrepid eye the dark domain of chaos; and without a moment's hesitation, spreading his vast wings, which could have covered a whole army, he flung himself into the abyss.

I'll leave the boldest among you to try and do as much. – And this is, in my view, one of the great efforts of the imagination, and one of the finest journeys ever undertaken, – next to the journey around my room.

38

I would never end if I tried to describe the thousandth part of the strange events that befall me when I start travelling near my library; the voyages of Cook and the observations of his travelling companions, Drs Banks and Solander,[27] are nothing in comparison with my adventures in this district alone: I therefore believe that I would spend my life there in a state of rapture, were it not for the bust I have mentioned, on which my eyes and my thoughts always end up being fixed, whatever the situation of my soul; and when she is too violently agitated, or succumbs to discouragement, I have only to look at this bust to restore her natural equilibrium: it is the *tuning fork* with which I tune the variable and discordant assembly of sensations and perceptions that forms my existence.

What a good likeness it is! – Those really are the features that nature had given to the most virtuous of men. Ah, if only the sculptor had managed to render visible his excellent soul, his genius and his character! – But what path have I embarked on here? Is this the place to sing his praises? Is it to the men who surround me that I am addressing myself? Ah, and what do *they* care?

I will content myself with prostrating myself before your cherished image, O best of fathers! Alas! This image is all that remains to me of you and of my native land: you departed this earth just as crime was about to overrun it; and such are the ills with which it assails us that your family itself is today forced to regard your death as a benefit. How many ills a longer life would have inflicted on you! O my father! Is the fate of your numerous family known to you in the realms of bliss? Do you know that your children are exiled from that native land that you served for sixty years with so much zeal and integrity? Do you know that they are forbidden to visit your tomb? – But tyranny has proved unable to strip them of the most precious part of your heritage: the memory of your virtues and the strength of your examples: in the midst of the tide of crime that was sweeping their land and their fortune into the abyss, they remained unalterably united and kept to the line you had traced out for them; and when they will again be able to prostrate themselves over your venerated ashes, those ashes will still be able to recognise them.

39

I promised a dialogue, and I will keep my word. – It was daybreak: the sun's rays were simultaneously gilding the summit of Mount Viso[28] and that of the highest mountains on the island at our antipodes; and already *she* was awake. Her early awakening was either the effect of the nocturnal visions that often throw her into an agitation as wearying as it is fruitless, or due to the fact that the carnival, which was drawing towards its end, had an occult effect on her, since that time of pleasure and folly may have an influence on the human machine, as do the phases of the moon and the conjunction of certain planets. – Anyway, *she* was awake, and wide awake, when my soul herself threw off the bonds of sleep.

For a long time my soul had confusedly been sharing the sensations of the *other*; but this soul of mine was still entangled in the veils of night and slumber; and these veils seemed to her to be transformed into gauze, into linen, into Indian cloth. – So my poor soul was, so to speak, enwrapped in all this adornment; and so as to keep her more firmly under his dominion, the god of sleep added to his bonds tresses of dishevelled blonde hair, knotted ribbons and pearl necklaces; anyone seeing her struggling within these nets would have felt pity for her.

The agitation felt in the noblest part of myself communicated itself to the other, and this part in turn acted powerfully on my soul. – My whole being had reached a state difficult to describe, when finally my soul, either through good sense or mere chance, found the right way to deliver herself from the layers of gauze that were suffocating her. I do not know if she found an opening, or simply decided to lift those gauze swathings, as seems more natural; the fact is that she found a way out of the labyrinth. The tresses of dishevelled hair were still there; but they were no longer an *obstacle*, but rather a *means*: my soul seized on it, as a drowning man clutches the weeds on the river-bank; but the pearl necklace broke in the tussle, and the pearls slipped off and rolled onto the sofa and thence onto Mme de Hautcastel's parquet floor; for my soul, through some strange quirk of imagination difficult to explain, thought that she was at that lady's house: a big bouquet of violets fell to the ground, and my soul, which thereupon awoke, returned home, bringing in her train reason and reality. As you can imagine, she strongly disapproved of everything that had been happening during her absence, and it's here that begins the dialogue that is the subject of this chapter.

Never had my soul met with such a poor reception. The reproaches that she took it into her head to utter at this critical juncture finally split up the couple: there was a rebellion, a veritable insurrection.

'What!' said my soul, 'so that's how it is: during my absence, instead of restoring your strength by having a peaceful sleep, and thereby making yourself more able to execute my orders, you have *insolently* decided' (the term was a bit strong) 'to succumb to transports of delight that my will had not sanctioned?'

Little accustomed to this haughty tone, *the other* flew into a rage, and retorted:

'Oh yes, you're a fine one, madam,' (since any idea of familiarity needed to be excluded from the discussion), 'you're a fine one to give yourself airs of decency and virtue! Ah, it's the whims of your imagination and your bizarre ideas that are responsible for everything about me that you most dislike! Why weren't you there? – Why should you have the right to go off and enjoy yourself without me, on those frequent journeys you make all by yourself? – Have I ever uttered a word of disapproval of your sessions in the empyrean or the Elysian Fields, your conversations with disembodied intelligences, your profound speculations,' (a touch of mockery, obviously), 'your castles in the air, your sublime systems? And why shouldn't I have the right, when you abandon me in this way, to enjoy the benefits that nature grants me and the pleasures she confers on me?'

My soul, taken aback at such vivacity and eloquence, did not know what to reply. – To settle matters, she attempted to cover with a veil of benevolence the rebukes that *she* had just permitted herself to make; and so as not to seem to be the one taking the first steps towards reconciliation, she also decided to affect a ceremonious tone. – 'Madam,' she said in turn, with an affected cordiality… (If the reader found this word out of place when it was being addressed to my soul, what will he say now, if he simply remembers the subject of the argument? – My soul did not sense the extreme ridiculousness of this way of speaking – so much does passion darken intelligence!)

'Madam,' she said, then, 'I can assure you that nothing would give me more pleasure than to see you enjoy all the pleasures of which your nature is capable, even if *I* do not share them – so long as those pleasures are not harmful and do not have a deleterious affect on the harmony that –'

Here my soul was suddenly and loudly interrupted.

'No, no, I'm not taken in by your apparent benevolence: – the enforced stay we are making together in this room through which we are travelling; the wound I have received, which has almost destroyed me, and is still bleeding; is not all this the fruit of your extravagant pride and your barbaric prejudices? My well-being and even my existence count for nothing when your passions start to drag you away, – and you pretend to have my interests at heart, and say that your rebukes stem from your friendship!'

My soul could easily see that she wasn't playing the most noble role on this occasion: – in any case, she was starting to realise that the heat of the quarrel had pushed its cause into the background, and, taking advantage of the circumstance to create a diversion, she told Joannetti, who had just come into the room, 'Make some coffee!' – The noise of the cups drew the full attention of the *insurgent*, and she immediately forgot everything else. It's just like when you show children a little toy, and thereby make them forget all about the unhealthy fruit they are jumping up and down to have.

I imperceptibly drowsed off as the water was boiling. – I was enjoying that charming pleasure which I have already described to my readers, the one you feel as you sense that you are going off to sleep. The agreeable noise that Joannetti made as he banged the coffee pot on the firedog echoed in my brain, and made all my sensitive fibres vibrate, just as striking a harp-string makes the octaves sound. – Finally, I saw a kind of shadow before me; I opened my eyes, it was Joannetti. Ah! What an aroma! What a nice surprise! Coffee! Cream! A pyramid of toast! – Dear Reader, do have some breakfast with me.

40

What a rich storehouse of enjoyment has kindly nature endowed on those men whose hearts are able to enjoy! And what a variety in those enjoyments! Who can count the innumerable nuances that distinguish different individuals and the different stages in life? The indistinct memory of the pleasures of my childhood still makes me quiver. Shall I try to depict the enjoyment that is felt by the young man whose heart is beginning to burn with all the fires of passion? At that happy age when you are as yet unaware even of the name of self-interest, ambition, hatred and all the shameful passions that degrade and torment mankind; during that age – which is, alas, all too brief! – the sun shines with a splendour that you never again encounter later on in life. The air is purer; – the fountains are more limpid and more fresh; – nature has an aura, and the bosky woods have paths that you cannot find once you have reached maturity. God! What perfumes those flowers emit! How delicious are those fruits! With what colours does dawn deck itself! – All women are lovable and faithful; all men are kind, generous and sensitive; wherever you go, you meet with cordiality, openness and disinterest; in the whole of nature you find nothing but flowers, virtues and pleasures.

Do not the agitation of love and the hope of happiness flood our hearts with sensations as vivid as they are varied?

The spectacle of nature, our ability to contemplate it both as a whole and in every detail, opens up an immense field of enjoyments for reason to explore. Soon the imagination, hovering over this ocean of pleasures, increases their quantity and their intensity; the different sensations unite and combine in order to form new ones; dreams of glory mingle with the palpitations of love; benevolence marches beside egotism, which offers it its hand; melancholy comes from time to time to cast its solemn dark veil over us, and change our tears into pleasure. – Finally, the perceptions of the mind, the sensations of the heart, the very memories of the senses, are inexhaustible sources of pleasure and happiness for man. – So there is no cause for anyone to be surprised that the noise Joannetti made when he knocked the coffee pot against the firedog, and the unexpected sight of a cup of cream, should have made such a vivid and agreeable impression on me.

41

I immediately put on my *travelling clothes*, having examined them with a complacent eye; and it was then that I resolved to write an ad hoc chapter in which I would describe them to the reader. The shape and usefulness of these clothes are generally well enough known, so I will discuss more particularly their influence on the spirit of travellers. – My winter travelling outfit is made of the warmest and softest fabric it has been possible for me to find; it completely envelops me from head to feet; and when I'm in my armchair, with my hands in my pockets and my head pulled down into the collar of my coat, I resemble the statue of Vishnu without feet and hands which you can see in Indian pagodas.

You may, if you wish, view the influence that I attribute to travelling clothes on the travellers who wear them as a mere prejudice; what I can say for certain in this respect is that it would appear to me just as ridiculous to take a single step of my journey around my room dressed in my uniform and with my sword at my side, as it would be to go out into social circles in a dressing gown. – When I see myself dressed in this way, according to the rigorous demands of pragmatics, not only would I not be capable of continuing on my journey, but I think that I wouldn't even be in a state to read what I have written hitherto, and even less to understand it.

But does this surprise you? Don't we see, every day, people who think they are ill because of the length of their beards, or because someone takes it into his head to decide that they don't look very well, and to tell them so? Clothes have such an influence on the minds of men that there are valetudinarians who feel much better when they see themselves in a new outfit and a powdered wig: you even find some who thus deceive the public and themselves by taking great care over their outfits; – they die, one fine morning, all rigged up, and their deaths cause quite a stir.

Sometimes, they forgot to give the Count of *** several days' notice that he was to stand guard: – a corporal would go to wake him up nice and early the very same day he was due to do so, and to give him this sad piece of news; but the idea of getting up straight away, putting on his gaiters and going out without having given it a moment's thought the day before, disturbed him so greatly that he preferred to have it announced that he was ill, and to stay at home. So he would put on his dressing gown and send his wigmaker away; this gave him a pale, sickly appearance that alarmed his wife and his entire family. – He really found that he looked *a bit off colour* on days like that.

He'd tell everyone that this was the case, partly to keep up the pretence, partly, too, because he actually thought it was so. – Imperceptibly, the influence of the dressing gown would do its work: the broth he had eaten, willingly or not, made him feel nauseous; soon his friends and relatives were sending for news of him; this was more than enough to send him to bed without further ado.

In the evening, Dr Ranson found that his pulse was *accelerated*, and ordered him to be bled the next day. If the period of his guard duty had gone on a month more, the patient would have succumbed.

Who could doubt the influence of travelling clothes on travellers, when you reflect that poor Count *** thought more than once that he was about to take a journey into the next world as a result of having put on his dressing gown for no good reason in this one?

42

I was sitting by my fire, after dinner, all wrapped up in my *travelling clothes*, and yielding quite willingly to their influence, as I awaited the time to set off, when the vapours of digestion, rising to my brain, so obstructed the passages by which ideas make their way there from my senses that all communication found itself intercepted; and just as my senses were no longer transmitting any ideas to my brain, the latter, in its turn, could no longer send out the electrical fluid that animates them, the fluid with which the ingenious Dr Valli resuscitates dead frogs.[29]

You will easily be able to imagine, after reading this preamble, why my head fell onto my chest, and how the muscles of the thumb and index finger of my right hand, no longer stimulated by this fluid, relaxed to the point where a volume of the works of Marquis Caraccioli[30] that I had been holding tightly between those two fingers fell from my grasp without my noticing, and slid onto the hearth.

I had just been receiving visitors, and my conversations with the people who had just left had centred on the death of the famous Dr Cigna[31], who had just passed away, and whose death was universally regretted: he was lively, hard-working, a good physician and a famous botanist. – The merits of this skilful man were occupying my thoughts; and yet – I told myself – if it were possible for me to mention the souls of all those he may have helped over into the other world, who knows if his reputation might not suffer a bit of a setback?

I was imperceptibly starting to formulate a little speech on medicine and the progress it has made since Hippocrates. – I was wondering if the famous personages of history who died in their beds, such as Pericles, Plato, the celebrated Aspasia[32] and Hippocrates himself, had died just like ordinary people, of some putrid, inflammatory or verminous fever; and whether they had been bled, and stuffed full of medicines.

But to say just why I thought of these four personages rather than of others would be quite impossible. – Who can explain a dream? All that I can say is that it was my soul that mentioned the doctor of Cos, the doctor of Turin, and the famous statesman who performed such fine deeds and such great misdeeds.

But as for his elegant lady friend, I humbly confess that it was *the other* who pointed her out. – However, when I think of it, I might be tempted to feel just a twinge of pride; it is clear, after all, that in this dream the balance in favour of reason was four to one. – This is a lot for a soldier of my age.

Be that as it may, while I was indulging in these reflections, my eyes finally closed, and I fell into a deep sleep; but as I closed my eyes, the image of the characters I had been thinking of remained painted on that fine canvas known as our *memory*, and as those images mingled in my mind with the idea of summoning up the dead, I soon saw, arriving one after the other, Hippocrates, Plato, Pericles, Aspasia and Dr Cigna with his wig.

I saw them all sit down on the seats still drawn up round the fire; Pericles alone remained standing so as to read the gazettes.

'If the discoveries you are telling me about were true,' said Hippocrates to the doctor, 'and if they had been as useful to medicine as you claim, I would have seen a decrease in the number of men who descend each day into the realm of darkness, and yet the list of them all, according to the registers of Minos – which I have verified myself – is every bit as long as before.'

Dr Cigna turned towards me.

'You have doubtless heard of these discoveries?' he said to me; 'you know of Harvey's discovery of the circulation of blood; and that of the immortal Spallanzani concerning digestion, of which we now know the whole mechanism?[33]' – And he drew up a long and detailed list of all the discoveries in the field of medicine, and the host of remedies that we owe to chemistry; he finally delivered an academic discourse in favour of modern medicine.

'Am I to believe,' I replied, 'that those great men are ignorant of everything you have just been telling them, and that their souls, freed from the shackles of matter, still find that there is something obscure in nature?'

'Ah, how deeply you are mistaken!' cried the proto-doctor of the Peloponnese; 'the mysteries of nature are hidden from the dead as well as from the living; he who created and directs all is the only one who knows the great secret which men strive in vain to uncover: this is what we learn for certain on the banks of the Styx; and believe you me,' he added, turning to the doctor, 'strip off that remaining bodily spirit that you have brought from the abode of mortals; and since the labours of a thousand generations and all the discoveries of men have not managed to prolong for a single instant their existence – since Charon transports the same number of shades across the river in his barque each day – let us no longer toil to defend an art which, among the dead with whom we dwell, would be of no use even to doctors.' – Thus spoke the famous Hippocrates, to my great astonishment.

Dr Cigna smiled; and, as spirits are quite incapable of rejecting evidence or concealing the truth, not only did he share Hippocrates' opinion, but he even confessed, blushing in the way that intelligences do, that he had always suspected as much.

Pericles, who had gone over to the window, heaved a great sigh, the cause of which I could easily guess. He was reading an issue of the *Moniteur*[34] announcing the decline in the arts and sciences; he saw illustrious scholars abandoning their sublime speculations to invent new crimes; and he shuddered on hearing a horde of cannibals comparing themselves to the heroes of noble Greece, when they could execute on the scaffold, without shame or remorse, venerable old men, women and children, and cold-bloodedly commit the most atrocious and the most futile crimes.

Plato, who had been listening to our conversation without uttering a word, on seeing that it had come to an abrupt and unexpected end, now spoke in his turn.

'I can understand,' he told us, 'that the discoveries made by your great men in all the branches of physics are useless to medicine, which will never be able to change the course of nature unless it be at the cost of men's lives; but the same can hardly be said, one would think, of the investigations that have been carried out into politics. Locke's discoveries about human nature, the invention of printing, the accumulated observations drawn from history, the countless profound books that have spread knowledge even among the people; – so many marvellous things, in short, must doubtless have contributed to making men better? And that wise and happy republic that I had imagined, and that the century in which I lived had led me to view as an impracticable dream, surely exists in the world of today?'

To this question, the honest doctor lowered his eyes; his only answer was his tears. Then, as he was wiping these away with his handkerchief, he accidentally pulled his wig askew, so that part of his face was hidden by it.

'Immortal gods!' said Aspasia, with a shriek; 'what a strange figure you cut! So is *that* one of your great men's discoveries – leading you to imagine you can wear another man's skull on your heads?'

Aspasia, yawning at the philosophers' speeches, had picked up a fashion magazine from the mantelpiece and had been leafing through it for some time, when the doctor's wig drew this exclamation from her; and as the narrow, wobbly seat on which she was sitting was very uncomfortable, she had quite unceremoniously stretched out her two bare legs, swathed in bands, on the straw-bottomed chair between herself and me, and had propped her elbow on one of Plato's broad shoulders.

'It's not a skull,' replied the doctor, taking his wig and throwing it on the fire. 'It's a wig, madam, and I don't know why I didn't throw that ridiculous adornment into the flames of Tartarus[35] when I arrived among you; but absurdities and prejudices are so inherent in our wretched nature that they continue to follow us for some time beyond the grave.'

I took a singular pleasure in seeing the doctor thus abjuring both his medicine and his wig.

'I can assure you,' Aspasia replied, 'that most of the hairdos depicted in the little book I have been leafing through deserve the same fate as yours – they are *so* outlandish!' – The lovely Athenian derived considerable amusement from looking through these engravings, and was justifiably amazed at the variety and bizarreness of modern fashions. One figure especially caught her attention: that of a young woman shown with one of the most elegant hairdos, which Aspasia merely found rather too high; but the gauze piece covering her neck and bosom was so extraordinarily wide that you could see hardly half of her face. Aspasia, unaware that these marvellous shapes were merely the result of the use of starch, could not hold back her astonishment, which would have been twice as intense – and her consternation twice as great – if the gauze had been transparent.

'But do please tell us,' she said, 'why the women of today seem to have clothes to conceal themselves in rather than to wear? They hardly reveal their faces, and by their faces alone can you recognise their sex, since the shapes of their bodies are so disfigured by the bizarre folds in the fabric! Of all the figures depicted in these pages, none displays her bosom, arms or legs: why haven't your young warriors tried to destroy such outfits? Apparently,' she went on, 'the virtue of the women of today, which is made plain to see in all the clothes they wear, must greatly surpass that of the women of my own day?'

As she concluded, Aspasia looked at me and seemed to be asking for a reply. – I pretended not to have noticed; – and, so as to give myself an air of distinction, I took the fire tongs and poked the remains of the doctor's wig that had been spared by the flames and were lying among the embers. – Then, noticing that one of the bands tying Aspasia's buskin had come undone, I said, 'Pardon me, my dear' – and, as I spoke, I quickly stooped down, reaching out towards the chair, where I thought I could catch a glimpse of those two legs that in bygone days had turned the wits of great philosophers.

I am convinced that, just at that moment, I must have been in a state close to somnambulism, since the movement of which I am telling you was perfectly real; but Rosine, who was in fact resting on the chair, took this movement as an invitation to her, and, leaping gracefully into my arms, sent the famous shades summoned by my travelling clothes back down to Hades.

Enchanting land of imagination, you whom the most benevolent Being bequeathed to men to console them for reality, I must leave you. – Today is the day when certain persons on whom I depend say they will restore me to freedom. As if they had taken freedom from me! As if it had been in their power to deprive me of it for a single moment, and to prevent me from exploring at will the vast space that always lies open before me! – They have forbidden me to roam around a city, a mere point in space; but they have left me with the whole universe: immensity and eternity are mine to command.

So, today is the day I am to be free, or rather the day on which I am to be shackled in chains once more! The yoke of business will once more weigh down on me; I will no longer be able to take a single step that is not traced out for me by propriety and duty. – I may still be happy if some capricious deity makes me forget both of them, and if I can escape from this new and dangerous captivity!

Ah, why didn't they let me finish my journey? Was it to punish me that they had locked me up in my room – in that delightful country that holds every good thing, and all the riches of life, within its realm? You may as well exile a mouse in a granary.

Nonetheless, never have I been more clearly aware that I am *double*. – While I yearn for my imaginary enjoyments, I feel perforce consoled; a secret power draws me on; – it tells me that I need the heaven's air, and that solitude resembles death. – So I am all dressed up; – my door opens; – I roam beneath the spacious porticoes of the road along the Po; a thousand agreeable phantoms flutter along in front of my eyes. – Yes, here's the building, – this door, these stairs; – I am filled with a premonitory shudder.

It's exactly the same as when you cut into a lemon to eat it, and feel an acidic taste already in your mouth.

O my beast, my poor beast, beware!

NOTES

1. Jean-Baptiste-Louis Gresset (1709–77) wrote a comic poem, *Vert-Vert*, about a parrot whose scabrous language shocked its owners, a group of nuns.
2. Nicole is a character in Molière's *Le Bourgeois Gentilhomme* (1660), a comedy which satirises the pretensions of M. Jourdain, a middle-class man who apes such aristocratic pastimes as fencing, in which 'quart' and 'tierce' are both parrying positions.
3. Jean-Baptiste Beccaria (1716–81) was a famous professor of physics at the University of Turin. The King of Sardinia commissioned him, in 1759, to measure a meridian degree in Piedmont. He published his results in 1774.
4. Charles Le Brun (1619–90) was chief painter to Louis XIV. One of his main interests lay in establishing a typology of facial expression and gesture.
5. Martinism was a romantic spiritualist doctrine developed by Louis-Claude de Saint-Martin (1743–1803).
6. The philosopher Empedocles, according to legend, threw himself into Mount Etna.
7. Charlotte, the wife of the staid civil servant Albert, is the object of Werther's doomed love in Goethe's *The Sorrows of Young Werther* (1774).
8. Count Ugolino and his two sons and grandsons were locked in a tower in Pisa by his enemy, Archbishop Ruggieri, where they starved to death (1289). The story is related by Dante (*Inferno*, Canto 33).
9. The Chevalier d'Assas became a byword for heroic self-sacrifice when he went down fighting, vastly outnumbered, in a skirmish in 1760.
10. As de Maistre goes on to make clear, this painting is *La Bergère des Alpes* (*The Shepherdess of the Alps*) by Claude-Joseph Vernet (1714–89). *Cacalia* is a genus of tall herbs, common in the forested mountains of Europe.
11. Uncle Toby's main hobby horse (in Laurence Sterne's novel *Tristram Shandy*) is the art of military fortification.
12. Domenico Cimarosa (1749–1801) was the composer of, among other things, the opera *Il matrimonio segreto*, much-loved by Stendhal; Luigi Cherubini (1760–1842) was also a composer (of some thirty operas and a famous *Requiem*, among other things).
13. Antonio Allegri Correggio (*c.*1490–1534), mannerist painter of the Parma school.
14. Apelles of Ionia (4th century BC) was considered the greatest painter of antiquity.
15. As was de Maistre himself.
16. *Casin* (or *casino*): a villa.
17. Luigi Marchesi, known as Marchesini (1754–1829), was a celebrated castrato singer and dandy.
18. The 1839 edition here included a note on Mlle Rapous: 'A celebrated seller of fashionable clothes at the time of *A Journey around my Room*, some thirty-three years ago'.
19. In Racine's play *Athalie* (1691), the eponymous queen has a terrifying and prophetic dream of her own violent death (Act III, scene V).
20. The Prisoner of Pignerol is better known as the Man in the Iron Mask.
21. The Castello del Valentino, near Turin.

22. Cleveland is a character in the novel by Abbé Prévost (1696–1763) that appeared in English in 1735 as *The Life and Entertaining Adventures of Mr Cleveland, Natural Son of Oliver Cromwell.*
23. The Abaquis were a North American tribe that feature in Prévost's novel.
24. The Ruintons appear in the same novel.
25. The Argonauts accompanied Jason on his expedition, aboard the *Argo*, to win the Golden Fleece at Colchis. The Assembly of Notables, slightly closer to de Maistre's home, was comprised of members of the privileged orders summoned to Versailles in 1787 by Charles-Alexandre de Calonne, who hoped (in vain) that they would carry through some moderate and much-needed reforms.
26. Ossian was the Irish warrior poet who became celebrated throughout Europe when, in 1762, James Macpherson (1736–96) published *Fingal,* claiming it was a translation from Ossian: it was in fact a pastiche of Gaelic ballads that became immensely influential in forming the romantic taste for the misty, heroic Celtic past.
27. Joseph Banks and the Swedish botanist Daniel Solander were scientists on board Captain Cook's HMS *Endeavour*. On his 1768–71 journey, they observed the transit of Venus from Tahiti (1769).
28. Monte Viso, in the western Alps, is visible from Turin and is the source of the Po.
29. Eusebio Valli (1755–1816) was a doctor who did indeed experiment with frogs, but who also performed heroic experiments with potential rabies vaccines that were eventually to lead to his death.
30. Louis-Antoine Caraccioli (1719–1803), a writer of Neapolitan origin and a fervent Catholic, was more favourable to contemporary Italy and the Papal dominions than most intellectuals of his day; for these reasons, and since he was critical of the Enlightenment, he probably appealed to de Maistre.
31. Gian Francesco Cigna (1734–90) was a celebrated anatomy professor active in Turin, where he co-founded what was to become the Royal Academy of Sciences.
32. Aspasia was an intellectual Athenian woman and mistress of Pericles.
33. Lazzaro Spallanzani (1729–99) was a scientist with wide-ranging interests – not just digestion, but microscopic life, transplantation and artificial insemination.
34. The *Moniteur universel* was founded in 1789 to publish the debates of the French Constituent Assembly.
35. See note 16 to *A Nocturnal Expedition around my Room.*

A Nocturnal Expedition around my Room

1

To make the new room in which I made a nocturnal expedition a little more interesting, I must tell the curious reader how I had come to own it. Continually distracted from my occupations in the noisy house where I was living, I had long been planning on finding for myself a more solitary retreat in the neighbourhood, when one day, as I was glancing through a biographical article on M. Buffon[1], I read that this celebrated man had chosen in his gardens an isolated pavilion, which contained no other furniture than the armchair and the desk on which he wrote, nor any work other than the manuscript on which he was labouring.

The fancies that I busy myself with are so completely different from the immortal works of M. Buffon that the thought of imitating him, even in spirit, would doubtless never have sprung to my mind, were it not for a certain accident that finally persuaded me to do so. As a servant was wiping the dust off the furniture, he thought he could see a great deal of it on a pastel painting I had just finished, and wiped it so energetically with a cloth, that he did indeed manage to rid it of all the dust that I had, with considerable care, arranged on it. Having flown into a rage against this man, who was no longer there, and having abstained from saying anything about it to him when he returned – as usual – I immediately put my plan into action, and came home with the key to a small room that I had rented on the fifth floor of a place in Providence Street. That same day, I had all the equipment I needed for my favourite occupations transported there, and subsequently spent the greater part of my time in it, far from domestic hustle and bustle and all those who enjoy cleaning pictures. Hours sped by like minutes in this isolated little spot, and more than once my theories absorbed me so much I forgot to notice when it was dinner-time.

O sweet solitude! I have known the charms with which you intoxicate your lovers. Woe betide the man who cannot go a single day in his life without feeling the torments of boredom, and who prefers, if need be, to converse with idiots rather than with himself!

Still, I will confess that, while I like solitude in big cities, unless I am forced by some grave circumstance, such as a journey around my room, it is only in the morning that I have a desire to be a hermit; in the evening, I like to see human faces. The drawbacks of social life and those of solitude thus cancel each other out, and these two modes of existence embellish each other mutually.

However, the inconstancy and inevitability of the things of this world are such that the very intensity of the pleasures I enjoyed in my new abode should have forewarned me that they would not last long. The French Revolution, spilling out on every side, had just flowed across the Alps, and was flooding through Italy. I was swept by the first wave as far as Bologna. I kept my hermitage, to which I had all my furniture moved, until happier times. For some years I had been without a native land; I learnt one fine morning that I was now without a job. After a whole year spent seeing men and things that I had little liking for, and longing for men and things that I could no longer see, I returned to Turin. I had to make a decision. I left the inn of the Good Lady, where I had at first lodged, with the intention of returning the little room to its proprietor and getting rid of my furniture.

On returning to my hermitage, I was overcome by sensations difficult to describe: everything there was still in the order – that is the disorder – in which I had left it: the furniture piled up against the walls had been preserved from dust by the height of my little refuge; my pens were still in the dried-up inkwell, and I found on the table a letter that I had begun to write.

'I'm still at home,' I told myself with a real feeling of satisfaction. Every object reminded me of some event in my life, and my room was swathed with memories. Instead of returning to the inn, I decided to spend the night amidst my own effects. I sent for my trunk, and at the same time resolved to leave the next day, without saying goodbye to anyone or seeking their advice, abandoning myself unreservedly to Providence.

2

While I was reflecting thus, and congratulating myself on a well-thought-out travel plan, time was going by, and my servant had still not returned. He was a man whom necessity had induced me to take into my service a few weeks previously, and of whose loyalty I had started to become suspicious. The idea that he might have made off with my trunk had hardly entered my mind before I had rushed over to the inn: there was still time. As I was turning the corner of the street on which the inn of the Good Lady is situated, I saw him hurrying out of the door, with a porter ahead of him carrying my trunk. He himself had picked up my travelling bag; and instead of turning in my direction, he was heading left, in the opposite direction to the one he should have been taking. His intention was starting to become clear. I easily caught up with him and, without saying a word, walked alongside him for some time before he noticed. If you had wished to paint the expression of surprise and alarm taken to their highest degree on a human face, he would have provided a perfect model when he saw me at his side. I had all the time in the world to study his face, since he was so disconcerted at my sudden appearance and at the serious air with which I was gazing at him that he continued to walk with me for a while without uttering a word, as if we had been out for a stroll together. Finally he stammered out his excuse – some business he had in Grand-Doire Street[2]; but I set him on the right road, and we returned home, where I dismissed him.

Only then did I decide to make a new journey around my room, in the course of the last night that I would be spending there, and I immediately busied myself with the preparations.

3

For a long time I had wanted to revisit the country that I had once explored with such delight, and the description of which was in my view still incomplete. A few friends who had enjoyed it were urging me to continue, and I would doubtless have resolved to do so earlier, if I had not been separated from my travelling companions. I was setting off reluctantly. Alas! I was setting off alone. I would be travelling without my dear Joannetti and without sweet Rosine. My first room itself had undergone the most disastrous revolution; worse than that, it no longer existed – its precincts were now part of a horrible, flame-blackened ruin, and all the murderous inventions of war had united to destroy it from top to bottom. The wall on which the portrait of Mme de Hautcastel had hung had been pierced by a cannon shot. Finally, if I hadn't been fortunate enough to embark on my journey before this catastrophe, today's scholars would never have known of this remarkable room. In the same way, without the observations of Hipparchus[3], they would be quite unaware today that there used to be an extra star in the Pleiades which has vanished since that famous astronomer saw it.

Already, forced by circumstances, I had for some time abandoned my room and taken my penates elsewhere. That's no big deal, people will say. But how can I replace Joannetti and Rosine? Ah! It's just not possible. Joannetti had become so necessary to me that nothing will ever make up for his loss. And then, who *can* flatter himself that he will always live with the people he loves? Similar to those swarms of little flies that you see spinning in the air on fine summer evenings, men meet by chance and for only a very short time. And they are lucky if, in their rapid movement, they are as skilful as the flies and don't dash their heads against each other!

One evening, I was going to bed. Joannetti was serving me with his ordinary zeal, and even seemed somewhat more attentive. When he took the light out, I glanced at him and saw a marked deterioration in his physiognomy. But was I supposed to deduce that this was the last time that poor Joannetti would be serving me? I will not keep the reader in an uncertainty even crueller than the truth. I prefer to tell him straight out that Joannetti got married that very same night, and left me the following day.

But let no one accuse him of ingratitude for having left his master so abruptly. I had long known of his intention, and I had been wrong to oppose it. An official came to my home early in the morning to give me this news, and I had plenty of time, before I saw Joannetti, to fly into a rage and calm down again, which meant he was spared the reproaches that he was expecting. Before coming into my room, he pretended to be talking to someone while still in the corridor, to make me think he wasn't afraid; and arming himself with all the effrontery that such a kindly soul as his could muster, he presented himself with an air of determination. I immediately saw on his face everything that was transpiring in his soul, and I wasn't cross with him. The people who, these days, are always sniggering about the dangers of marriage have so intimidated decent folk that a newly wed man often resembles someone who has just taken a terrible tumble without hurting himself, and who is overcome with simultaneous alarm and satisfaction – which makes him look ridiculous. So it wasn't surprising that the actions of my faithful servant should reflect the strangeness of his situation.

'So, I gather you're married, my dear Joannetti?' I asked him with a laugh. He had summoned up his strength to face my wrath and now found that all his preparations had been a waste of time. He suddenly relapsed into his ordinary frame of mind, and even sank a little lower: indeed, he started to cry.

'What do you expect, sir?' he asked me, sobbing. 'I'd given my word.'

'And dammit, you did just the right thing, my friend! I hope you'll be happy with your wife, and especially with yourself! May you have children just like you! So, we're going to have to go our separate ways!'

'Yes, sir; we're intending to go and settle in Asti[4].'

'And when do you want to leave me?'

At this point Joannetti lowered his eyes, looking embarrassed, and replied a whole two tones lower, 'My wife has found a wagoner from her part of the world who's going back home with his wagon empty. He's leaving today. It would be a really good opportunity; but...

well… I'll go when sir is ready… though it will be difficult to find such an opportunity again.'

'What? So soon?' I replied. A sentiment of regret and affection, mixed with a strong dose of resentment, kept me silent for a while. 'No, certainly,' I said to him, somewhat harshly, 'don't let me keep you back; you can leave this very minute, if that's the best thing for you.'

Joannetti went pale.

'Yes, my friend, you run off after your wife; always be as kind and honest as you have been with me.'

We sorted out a few things, and I bade him a sad farewell. He left.

This man had served me for fifteen years. An instant separated us. I've never seen him again.

I was brooding over this abrupt separation as I walked up and down in my room. Rosine had followed Joannetti without him noticing. A quarter of an hour later, the door opened; Rosine came in. I saw Joannetti's hand pushing her into the room; the door closed, and I felt my heart contract… 'Already he won't set foot in my room!' I thought. – 'A few minutes have sufficed to estrange from one another two old companions who'd been together for fifteen years. Oh sad, sad condition of humanity, never able to find a single stable object on which to set the least of its affections!'

4

Rosine, too, was living far away from me. It will no doubt interest you to know, my dear Marie, that at the age of fifteen she was still the most lovable of animals, and that the same superiority of intelligence that had once distinguished her from her entire species also enabled her to bear the burden of old age. I would have preferred not to be separated from her; but when it comes to the fate of our friends, should we consult only our own pleasure or interest? It was in Rosine's interest to leave the itinerant life that she had been leading with me, and to enjoy at last, in her old age, a repose that her master could no longer hope for. Her great age obliged me to have her carried. I felt it was my duty to grant her these invalid benefits. A kindly disposed nun promised to look after her for the rest of her days; and I know that in her retirement she enjoyed all the advantages that she had deserved thanks to her good qualities, her age and her reputation.

And since the nature of men is such that happiness does not seem made for them, since friend unwittingly offends friend, and even lovers cannot live without quarrelling – in short, since from Lycurgus[5] to our own days all legislators have failed in their efforts to make men happy – I will at least have the consolation of having made a dog happy.

5

Now that I have informed my readers of the last details in the story of Joannetti and Rosine, I simply need to say a word about the soul and the beast: it is my duty to do so. These two personages, the latter one in particular, will no longer be playing such an interesting role in my journey. An amiable traveller who has followed the same path as myself claims that they must be feeling tired. Alas, he is too right! It's not that my soul has lost any of her activity, at least as far as she can tell; but her relations with *the other* have changed. The latter no longer has the same vivacity in her repartee; she no longer has – how shall I put it?... – I was going to say the same presence of mind, as if a beast could have a mind! Anyway, without going into a tangled explanation, I'll merely say that, led on by the trust in me that the young Alexandrine had demonstrated, I had written her quite an affectionate letter, when I received from her a polite but frigid reply that finished in these very terms: 'You can be sure, sir, that I will always harbour sentiments of the most sincere esteem for you.'

'Heavens above!' I straight away exclaimed. 'I'm doomed!'

Since that fateful day, I resolved to stop proposing my system of the soul and the beast. In consequence, without distinguishing between these two beings and without separating them, I will make them travel one on top of the other, as certain merchants do with their merchandise, and I will travel en bloc to avoid any inconvenience.

6

There wouldn't be any point in talking about the dimensions of my new room. It is so much like the earlier one that, at first glance, you would think it was the same – if, thanks to a precaution taken by the architect, the ceiling didn't slope towards the street, leaving the roof to face the way demanded by the laws of hydraulics so as to drain off the rain. My room gets its daylight from a single opening two and a half feet wide and four feet high, raised some six to seven feet above the floor: you can reach it with a small ladder.

The elevation of my window above the floor was one of the lucky circumstances that could have been due either to chance or to the genius of the architect. The almost perpendicular light that it shed into my little den gave it a mysterious feel. The ancient temple of the Pantheon is lit in more or less the same way. Furthermore, there was no external object to distract me. Like those navigators who, lost on the vast ocean, can see nothing but sea and sky, I could see nothing but the sky and my room, and the nearest external objects on which my gaze could fall were the moon or the morning star: this gave me an immediate sense of rapport with the sky, and gave my thoughts an elevated flight that they would never have had if I had chosen my lodgings on the ground floor.

The window I just mentioned rose above the roof and formed the prettiest skylight: it was so far above the horizon that when the sun's first rays came to illumine it, darkness still reigned down in the street. As a result I enjoyed one of the most beautiful vistas that anyone can imagine. But even the most beautiful vista soon wearies you when you see it too often; your eye gets used to it, and you don't appreciate it any more. The position of my window protected me from this drawback, since I could never see the magnificent spectacle of the Turin countryside without climbing four or five rungs on my ladder, which procured for me joys that were always intense, since I indulged in them sparingly. When, feeling tired, I wanted to give myself a pleasant little break, I would end my journey by climbing up to my window.

On the first rung, I could see only the sky; soon the colossal temple of Superga[6] came into view. The hill of Turin, on which it rests, gradually rose before me, covered with forests and rich vineyards, displaying its gardens and palaces proudly to the setting sun, while its simple and modest dwellings seemed half hidden away in those little valleys, serving as a retreat for the wise man whose meditations they could foster.

Charming hill! You have often seen me seeking out your solitary retreats, and preferring your isolated paths to the brilliant thoroughfares of the capital; you have often seen me lost amid your labyrinths of verdure, attentive to the song of the dawn lark, my heart full of vague disquiet and the ardent desire to settle for good in your enchanted valleys! – I salute you, charming hill! You are painted within my heart! May the dew of heaven make, if possible, your fields more fertile and your bosky woods more leafy! May your inhabitants enjoy their happiness in peace, and your shade be favourable and salutary to them! May, finally, your happy land always be a sweet refuge for true philosophy, modest science, and the sincere and hospitable friendship that I have found there!

7

I began my journey at eight in the evening precisely. The weather was calm and promised a fine night ahead. I had taken precautions not to be disturbed by visits – they are extremely rare at the height at which I was living, and especially in the circumstances in which I then found myself – and counted on remaining alone until midnight. Four hours gave me ample time to carry out my plan, since on this occasion I merely wanted to perform a simple excursion around my room. If the first journey lasted forty-two days, this was because I hadn't been in any position to ensure that it took a shorter time. Nor did I wish to be constrained to travelling much in a coach, as before, since I am convinced that a traveller on foot sees many things that escape a man who travels with the post. So I decided to go on foot and on horseback alternately, depending on the circumstances: a new method which I have not yet revealed, and whose usefulness will soon be apparent. Finally, I resolved to take notes en route, and to write down my observations as and when I made them, so as not to forget anything.

So as to put my enterprise in shape, and give it an increased chance of success, I reflected that it would be good to begin by composing a dedicatory epistle, and writing it in verse to make it more interesting. But two difficulties caused me some perplexity and almost made me give up, despite all the benefits I could derive from the project. The first was knowing to whom I should address the epistle, the second, how on earth I should go about writing verse. On mature reflection, it didn't take me long to realise that the sensible thing would be to write my epistle first, as best I could, and then to find someone it might suit. I immediately settled down to work, and laboured for over an hour without being able to find a rhyme for the first line of verse I had composed, and that I wanted to preserve, since it struck me as quite inspired. Then I remembered, appropriately enough, having read somewhere that the celebrated Pope[7] never composed anything of interest without being obliged to declaim long and loud, and to walk energetically round and round his room so to stir up his creative juices. Thereupon, I tried to imitate him. I took the poetry of Ossian and recited it aloud, striding up and down so as to raise myself to a pitch of enthusiasm.

And I soon saw that this method did indeed imperceptibly exalt my imagination, and gave me a secret sense of my poetic capabilities which I would certainly have turned to good advantage, going on to compose my dedicatory verse epistle with great success, if I hadn't unfortunately forgotten the fact that the ceiling of my room sloped down: its sudden descent prevented my forehead from travelling forward the same distance as my feet in the direction I had taken. I banged my head against that wretched sloping ceiling so hard that the roof of the house was given quite a jolt: the sparrows who had been asleep under the tiles flew off in alarm, and the collision made me take three steps backwards.

8

Whilst I was walking around in this way to stimulate my imagination, a pretty young woman who was living below me, surprised at the noise I was making, and thinking perhaps that I was throwing a ball in my room, made her husband come up to find out what had caused the noise. I was still quite stunned by the contusion I had suffered, when the door half opened. An elderly man, wearing a melancholy expression, stuck his head in, and allowed his gaze to wander around the room. When his surprise at finding me alone had faded, he finally said, in vexed tones, 'My wife has a migraine, sir. Allow me to point out to you that…'

I immediately interrupted him, and my style reflected the sublimity of my thoughts.

'Worthy messenger of my lovely neighbour,' I told him in proper bardic style, 'why do your eyes gleam beneath your bushy eyebrows, like two meteors in the black forest of Cromba? Your beautiful partner is a ray of light, and I would die a thousand times over rather than deliberately disturb her repose; but your expression, O worthy messenger… your expression is as grim as the most remote recess in the cave of Camora, when the great and lofty clouds of the tempest cover the face of night, and weigh down on the silent countryside of Morven.'[8]

My neighbour, who had apparently never read Ossian's poetry, unfortunately took the outburst of divine inspiration that had overpowered me for an attack of madness, and seemed really perplexed. Since I had no intention of offending him, I offered him a seat and asked him to sit down; but I realised he was slowly beating a retreat, making the sign of the cross over himself as he murmured, '*È matto, per Bacco, è matto!*'[9]

9

I let him go, without seeking to determine how far his observation was well founded; I sat down at my desk to make a note of these events, as is my wont; but hardly had I opened a drawer in which I hoped I'd find some paper than I closed it abruptly, disturbed by one of the most disagreeable sentiments you can ever experience: that of humiliated self-esteem. The kind of surprise that overwhelmed me on this occasion resembles that which a thirsty traveller feels when, lowering his lips to a limpid fountain, he sees in the depths of the water a frog gazing at him. But in fact it was nothing other than the springs and the carcass of an artificial dove which, following the example of Archytas[10], I had once planned to send flying through the air. I'd worked unremittingly on its construction for over three months. When the day came for its test flight, I placed it on the edge of a table, after taking care to shut the door, so as to keep my discovery secret and spring an agreeable surprise on my friends. A thread was holding the mechanism immobile. Who could imagine the palpitations of my heart and the anguish of my self-esteem when I brought the scissors up to cut the fateful bond?... Swish!... The dove's spring uncoiled noisily. I looked up to see it take wing; but after turning round and round a few times, it fell down and went to hide under the table. Rosine, who was asleep there, sadly padded off. Rosine, who could never set eyes on a chicken, or a pigeon, or the least little bird, without attacking them and chasing after them, did not even deign to spare a glance for my dove, which was feebly fluttering on the floor... This dealt the *coup de grâce* to my self-esteem. I went out onto the ramparts for a bit of fresh air.

10

Such was the fate which befell my artificial dove. While the genius of mechanics had destined it to follow the eagle through the skies, destiny had given it the inclinations of a mole.

I was walking along, feeling sad and discouraged, as you always are after some great hope has been dashed, when, looking up, I noticed a flight of cranes passing over my head. I stopped to examine them. They were advancing in a triangular formation, like the English column at the Battle of Fontenoy.[11] I saw them flying across the sky, from cloud to cloud.

'Ah, how well they fly!' I murmured to myself; 'with what assurance they seem to glide along the invisible pathway they follow!'

Do I dare to admit it? Alas, may I be forgiven! The horrible emotion of envy has only ever once, on one single occasion, entered my heart, and it was an envy of cranes. I followed them with my jealous eyes to the limits of the horizon. For a long time, standing immobile amidst the crowd of strollers, I observed the rapid flight of the swallows, and I was amazed to see them hanging in the air, as if I had never seen this phenomenon before. A sense of profound admiration, of a kind I had never before experienced, lit up my soul. I thought I was beholding nature for the very first time. I was surprised to hear the buzzing of the flies, the song of the birds, and that mysterious, indistinct hubbub of the whole living creation as it spontaneously celebrated its author. An ineffable concert, to which man alone has the sublime privilege of being able to add a note of gratitude!

'Who is the author of this brilliant mechanism?' I exclaimed in a transport of delight. 'Who is he who, opening his creative hand, let the first swallow take wing into the air? – He who ordered these trees to rise up out of the earth and raise their branches heavenwards? – And you, who advance majestically in their shade, you ravishing creature whose face imposes respect and love! Who placed you on the earth's surface to beautify it? Whose mind was it that drew your divine shape, and was mighty enough to create the smile and the gaze of innocent beauty?... And I myself, as I feel my heart beating... what is the aim of my existence? – Who am I, and where do I come from – I, the maker of the centripetal artificial dove?'

Hardly had I pronounced this last barbarous phrase than, suddenly coming to my senses like a sleeping man who has a bucket of water thrown over him, I noticed that several people had surrounded me to examine me, while my enthusiasm was making me talk out loud. Then I saw the lovely Georgine, who was walking a few steps ahead of me. Half her left cheek, with its layer of rouge, was just visible through the curls of her blonde wig, and this finally brought me back down to earth, after my short absence.

11

As soon as I had recovered a little from the shock of seeing what had happened to my artificial dove, the pain of the contusion I had suffered really started to hurt. I passed my hand over my forehead, and recognised a new protuberance at exactly that part of the head where Dr Gall situates the bump of poetry.[12] But the thought did not cross my mind at the time, and only experience was to show me the truth of that great man's system.

After gathering my wits for a few moments so as to make one last effort on my dedicatory epistle, I picked up a pencil and settled down to work. How amazed I was!… The lines of poetry came flowing from my pen of their own accord; I filled two pages in less than an hour, and I concluded from this circumstance that, if movement was necessary for Pope's brain to compose poetry, nothing less than a contusion was required to extract it from mine. I will refrain, however, from presenting the poetry I then composed to the reader, since the extraordinary rapidity with which the adventures of my journey succeeded one another prevented me from putting the final touch to it. Despite this reticence on my part, there's no doubting that the accident which had befallen me should be regarded as a valuable discovery, one of which poets can never avail themselves too often.

I am so convinced of the infallibility of this new method, in fact, that as regards the poem in twenty-four cantos that I composed – it is to be published together with *The Prisoner of Pignerol*[13] – I have not thought it necessary until now to actually start putting it into rhyme; but I've written up five hundred pages of notes, which comprise, as everyone knows, all the merit, and fill out all the bulk, of most modern poems.

As I was deeply pondering my discoveries, walking up and down in my room, I ended up in front of my bed, on which I sat down heavily, and as my hand chanced to fall on my sleeping cap, I decided to put it on my head and go to bed.

12

I'd been in bed for a quarter of an hour, and, unusually for me, I still hadn't fallen asleep. The idea of my dedicatory epistle had been succeeded by the most sombre reflections: my candle, which was almost burnt out, now threw but a wavering and mournful flicker from the base of its wick, and my room seemed like a tomb. A gust of wind suddenly flung open the window, blew out my candle and slammed the door shut with a bang. The dark cast of my thoughts increased with the gloom.

All my past pleasures and all my present pains came to blend together within my heart, and filled it with bitterness and regret.

Although I am continually striving to forget my sorrows and to chase them from my thoughts, it sometimes happens, when I am not sufficiently on my guard, that they suddenly all come flooding into my memory at the same time, as if the sluice gates had been opened for them. On these occasions, I have no option but to abandon myself to the torrent sweeping me away, and my ideas then become so gloomy, and all the objects around me seem so dismal, that I usually end up laughing at my own folly; as a result, the very intensity of the malady produces its own remedy.

I was still facing the full force of one of these melancholy crises when part of the gust of wind that had blown open my window and slammed shut my door as it swept by, having roamed around my room several times, flicked through my books and swept a loose leaf from the account of my journey to the ground, fluttered through my curtains and came to expire on my cheek. I felt the welcome freshness of the night, and regarding all this as an invitation from it, I immediately got up, and climbed my ladder to enjoy the tranquillity of nature.

13

The sky was clear; the Milky Way, like a wispy cloud, ran across the middle of the sky, a gentle ray of light from every star shone down on me, and when I examined one of these stars attentively, its companions seemed to sparkle more vividly so as to draw my gaze.

The contemplation of the starry sky is a charm that never loses its novelty for me, and I need not reproach myself for ever having made a single journey, or even a single night-time stroll, without paying the tribute of admiration that I owe to the marvels of the firmament. Although I fully feel the impotence of my mind in these lofty meditations, I draw an inexpressible pleasure in busying myself with them. I love reflecting that it is not chance which is bringing to my eyes that emanation from far-off worlds, and each star sheds, with its light, a ray of hope into my heart. Ah, could it be that these marvels have no relation with me other than the fact that they shine before my eyes? And my mind which rises up to them, my heart which is moved by the sight of them – could they be strangers to the stars?... Man, the ephemeral spectator of an eternal spectacle, raises for an instant his eyes to the heavens, and then closes them again for ever; but, during this fleeting instant that is granted him, from every point of the sky and from the very furthest bourns of the universe, a consoling ray of light sets out from every world, and falls onto his eyes, announcing to him that there is a relationship between that immensity and himself, and that he is an associate of eternity.

14

However, a bothersome thought disturbed the pleasure I was experiencing as I indulged in these meditations. 'How few people,' I told myself, 'are now enjoying with me the sublime spectacle that the heavens spread out, in vain, for drowsy men!... Those who actually are asleep are one thing; but what would it cost those people out for a stroll, or those others emerging in crowds from the theatre, to look up for a moment and admire the brilliant constellations that are shining down on their heads from every direction? – No, the attentive spectators of Scapin or Jocrisse[14] will never deign to lift up their eyes: they will stump off like brutes back to their homes, or wherever they are going, without reflecting that the heavens exist. How very strange!... Since they can see the sky so often, and all for free, they can't be bothered with it. If the firmament were always veiled to us, if the spectacle it offers us depended on some entrepreneur, the best boxes in the rooftop theatre would be quite unaffordable, and the ladies of Turin would be fighting over my skylight.

'Oh, if I were the sovereign of some country,' I exclaimed, filled with righteous indignation, 'every night I would have the alarm bell rung, and I would oblige my subjects of every age, every sex, and every condition, to go to their windows and look at the stars.' At this point, Reason, which in my kingdom has only a limited right of remonstrance, was nonetheless more successful than usual in pointing out how unprecedented was the over-hasty edict that I wished to proclaim in my states.

'Sire,' she told me, 'might Your Majesty not deign to make an exception for rainy nights, since, in that case, the sky is overcast?...'

'Very well, very well,' I replied. 'I hadn't thought of that: you can take note that an exception will be made on rainy nights.'

'Sire,' she added, 'I think it might be a good idea to make an exception for nights when the sky is clear too, when the cold is excessive and there's a chill breeze blowing, since the rigorous application of the edict would bring down colds and catarrhs on your fortunate subjects.'

I was starting to see that there would be many difficulties in carrying out my plan; but I was reluctant to backtrack.

'We will need,' I said, 'to write to the Medical Council and the Academy of Sciences to fix the temperature, in degrees centigrade, at which my subjects can be dispensed from having to look out of the window; but I wish – no, I demand absolutely that the order be rigorously applied.'

'And what about those who are ill, sire?'

'That goes without saying; they can all be excepted; humanity must come before all else.'

'If I did not fear tiring Your Majesty, I would point out, in addition, that it might be possible (in cases when it was judged relevant and the thing did not present any great inconvenience) to make an additional exception in favour of the blind, since, being deprived of the organs of sight...'

'Well, is that all?' I interrupted in an ill humour.

'Forgive me, sire; but what about lovers? Could Your Majesty's merciful heart force them also to look at the stars?'

'All right, all right,' said the King; 'we'll come back to that some other time; we'll sleep on it first. You can give me a detailed memo all about it.'

Good Lord!... Good Lord!... how hard you need to think before you can issue an edict of State policy!

15

The most brilliant stars have never been the ones that I contemplate with the most pleasure; no, the smallest ones, those which, lost in incommensurable remoteness, appear no more than imperceptible points, have always been my favourites. The reason is quite simple: you will easily understand that, as I make my imagination travel as far beyond their sphere as my gaze travels to reach them from here, I am effortlessly conveyed to a distance which few travellers before me have reached, and I am astonished, when I find myself there, that I am still only at the beginning of this vast universe; for it would, I believe, be ridiculous to think that there is some barrier after which there is mere nothingness, as if nothingness were easier to comprehend than existence! After the last star, I can imagine another one, which cannot be the last one either. If we assign limits to creation, however remote those limits may be, the universe appears to me no more than a glowing point in comparison with the immensity of empty space surrounding it, that dark and dreadful void in the midst of which it seems suspended like a solitary lamp. – At this point I covered my eyes with my two hands, to keep any form of distraction at bay, and to give my ideas the profundity that such an object demanded; and, making a supernatural mental effort, I composed a system of the world, the most complete that has ever yet appeared. Here it is in all its details; it's the result of my lifetime meditations. 'I believe that, as space is…' But this requires a chapter to itself; and, seeing the importance of the subject, it will be the only chapter of my journey to bear a title.

16

The system of the world

I believe, then, that as space is finite, creation is also finite, and that God has created in his eternity an infinity of worlds in the immensity of space.

17

I will confess, however, in all good faith, that I don't really understand my system any better than all the other systems that have hitherto been hatched by the imaginations of ancient and modern philosophers; but mine has the precious advantage of being contained within a couple of lines, however vast it may be. The indulgent reader will also be good enough to observe that it was composed, in its entirety, at the top of a ladder. I would, however, have embellished it with commentaries and notes if, at the very time when I was the most intently occupied on my subject, I had not been distracted by enchanting sounds that came to strike agreeably on my ear. A voice more melodious than any I had ever heard, not even excepting that of Zénéide,[15] one of those voices that always vibrate in unison with the fibres of my heart, was singing nearby a romance of which I caught every word, and which will never depart from my memory. As I attentively listened, I discovered that the voice was coming from a window below mine: unfortunately I couldn't see it, since the edge of the roof, over which my skylight rose, hid it from my sight. However, my desire to catch sight of the siren who was charming me with her harmonies increased in proportion with the charm of the romance, whose poignant words would have drawn tears from the most insensitive creature. Soon, no longer able to resist my curiosity, I climbed up to the last rung, set one foot on the edge of the roof, and in this way, clinging with one hand to the side of the window, hung out over the street, at the risk of falling down.

Then I saw on a balcony to my left, a little lower down from me, a young woman in a white negligee: her hand was propping up her charming head, which was leaning forward sufficiently for me to make out, in the starlight, the most alluring profile, and her posture seemed tailor-made to present, as fully and clearly as possible, to an aerial traveller such as myself, a slender and attractive figure; one of her bare feet, casually flung backwards, was turned in such a way that I was able, despite the darkness, to guess at its lovely shape, while a pretty little slipper, which had become detached from it, gave it an even more precise form in my curious eyes. I leave you to imagine, my dear Sophie, how intense my situation was. I didn't dare utter the least exclamation, for fear of startling my lovely neighbour, nor the least movement, for fear of falling down into the street. However, a sigh escaped me in spite of myself; but I was in time to half suppress it; the rest was carried away by a passing zephyr, and I could examine the dreamy young lady at leisure, kept as I was in this perilous position by the hope of hearing her sing again. But alas! her romance was finished, and my unhappy destiny made her keep the most obstinate silence. Finally, after waiting for quite a while, I thought I could venture to say a word or two to her: all I needed was to dream up some compliment worthy of her and the feelings she had inspired in me. Oh, how bitterly I regretted not having finished my dedicatory verse epistle! How useful it would have come in on this occasion! My presence of mind did not abandon me at my moment of need. Inspired by the sweet influence of the stars and by the even more powerful desire to succeed with a beautiful girl, I gave a slight cough to attract her attention, and to make the sound of my voice more gentle, I said to her, in the most affectionate tone of voice I could manage, 'Lovely weather tonight!'

18

At this point I imagine Mme de Hautcastel, who never lets me off the hook, asking me for the romance I mentioned in the last chapter. For the first time in my life, I find myself in the necessity, harsh as it may be, of refusing her something. If I were to insert this poem into my journey, people wouldn't fail to deduce that I was the author, which would bring down on my head more than one sly joke on the need for contusions – something I prefer to avoid. So I will continue the story of my adventure with my dear neighbour, an adventure whose unexpected catastrophe, as well as the delicacy with which I conducted it, is bound to interest every class of reader. But, before knowing what she replied, and how she took the ingenious compliment I had addressed to her, I must reply in advance to certain persons who think they are more eloquent than I am, and who mercilessly condemn me for having struck up the conversation in such a trivial way – in their view. I will prove to them that, if I had started to be witty on this important occasion, I would have flagrantly disregarded the rules of prudence and good taste. Any man who embarks on a conversation with a beautiful woman by coming out with a witty remark or turning a compliment, however flattering it might be, shows a glimpse of intentions that should not become explicit until they are starting to be justified. Furthermore, if he starts being witty, it is clear that he is trying to shine, and thus that he is thinking less of the lady than of himself. Now, ladies always want you to focus on *them*; and although they don't always make the same reflections that I have just written down, they possess a natural and exquisite sense that teaches them that a trivial phrase, uttered with the sole intent of striking up a conversation and getting close to them, is worth a thousand times more than a witty sally inspired by vanity, and even more (though this may appear quite surprising) than a dedicatory epistle in verse. What's more, I maintain (even though my feeling may be regarded as paradoxical) that the light and brilliant wit of conversation is not even necessary in the most long-lasting love affair, if it has really sprung from the heart; and despite everything that those who have only ever half loved may say of the long intervals that intense feelings of love and friendship leave between them, the day always goes by quickly when you spend it with your beloved, and silence is as full of interest as any discussion.

* * *

Whatever you think of my little speech, it's a certain fact that I couldn't think of anything better to say, on the edge of the roof where I found myself, than the words in question. No sooner had I uttered them than my soul betook itself entire to the tympanum of my ears, to grasp the least little nuance of the sounds I hoped to hear. The lovely girl lifted her head to look up at me: her long hair unfolded like a veil, and served as a backdrop to her charming face, which reflected the mysterious light of the stars. Already her mouth was half open, and her sweet words were on the tip of her tongue... But Heavens above! What was my surprise and my terror!... A sinister noise made itself heard: 'Madam, what are you doing out there! At this time of the night! Come back in!' said a loud, masculine voice, from within the apartment. I was petrified.

19

The noise was like that which must terrify the guilty when the burning gates of Tartarus are suddenly flung open before them; or like that made, beneath the vaults of Hades, by the seven cataracts of the Styx, which the poets omitted to mention.[16]

20

A will-o'-the-wisp was shooting across the sky just then, only to disappear almost straight away. My eyes, which the bright flash of the meteor had momentarily distracted, returned to the balcony, and all they could see there was the little slipper. My neighbour, in her hasty withdrawal, had forgotten to pick it up. I gazed for a long time at this pretty shape, made to mould a foot worthy of the chisel of Praxiteles[17], with an emotion whose full strength I dare not admit; but what might appear quite singular, and what I could not explain to myself, is that an invincible charm prevented me from taking my eyes off it, despite all the efforts I made to look at other objects.

It is said that, when a snake gazes at a nightingale, the unfortunate bird, the victim of an irresistible fascination, is forced to approach the voracious reptile. Its swift wings now serve only to lead it to its destruction, and every effort it makes to get away merely brings it closer to the enemy who is pursuing it with a mesmerising gaze.

Such was the effect that this slipper had on me, though without my being able to say for sure which, out of me and the slipper, was the snake, since according to the laws of physics the attraction must have been reciprocal. It is certain that this fateful influence was no whim of my imagination. I was so truly and strongly attracted that I was twice on the verge of losing my grip and letting myself fall. However, as the balcony which I wanted to get to was not exactly under my window, but a little to one side, I could clearly see that the force of attraction invented by Newton would have combined with the oblique attraction of the slipper, so that in my fall I would have followed a diagonal line, and fallen onto a sentry box that, from the height at which I found myself, seemed to me no bigger than an egg. As a result, I would have missed my aim… So I gripped the window even more tightly, and, making a resolute effort, I managed to lift my eyes and gaze upon the sky.

21

I would find it difficult to explain and define exactly the kind of pleasure that I experienced at this juncture. All I can say is that it had nothing in common with the pleasure that the sight of the Milky Way and the starry sky had given me a few moments earlier. However, since in the most perplexing situations of my life I have always liked to be able to explain to myself what is transpiring in my soul, on this occasion I wanted to form a clear and distinct idea of the pleasure that can be felt by a decent chap when he is gazing at a lady's slipper, compared with the pleasure afforded him by the contemplation of the stars. To this end, I chose the constellation in the sky that was most clearly visible. It was, if I'm not mistaken, Cassiopeia's W above my head, and I looked in turn at the constellation and the slipper, and the slipper and the constellation. I then saw that these two sensations were quite different in nature; the one was in my head, while the other seemed to me to have its seat in the region of the heart. But what I cannot admit without a certain shame is that the allure attracting me towards the enchanted slipper absorbed all my faculties. The enthusiasm aroused in me, a short while before, by the sight of the starry sky now existed but feebly, and soon it evaporated altogether, when I heard the door to the balcony being reopened, and I spotted a little foot, whiter than alabaster, advancing slowly and fitting itself into the little slipper. I wanted to say something; but, not having had time to prepare myself as before, I could not find my usual presence of mind, and I heard the door to the balcony closing again before I could dream up something suitable to say.

22

The previous chapters will be enough, I hope, to constitute a victorious rebuttal of any incriminations made by Mme de Hautcastel, who did not refrain from denigrating my first journey, on the pretext that it afforded no opportunity for lovemaking. She couldn't make the same criticism of this new journey; and although my adventure with my dear neighbour didn't manage to be taken any further, I can assure her that I derived more satisfaction from it than in more than one other situation in which I had imagined I was bringing things to a happy conclusion, for lack of anything to compare it with. Everyone enjoys life in his or her own way; but I would feel that I was failing in my duty to the reader's benevolence if I did not inform him of a discovery which, more than anything else, has hitherto contributed to my happiness (so long, that is, as this remains our little secret); for what we have here is nothing less than a new way of making love, much more advantageous than the previous one, and with none of its disadvantages. As this invention was specially designed for the people who would like to adopt my new way of travelling, I feel I should devote a few chapters to instructing them in it.

I had observed, during the course of my life, that when I was in love in the usual way, my sensations never lived up to my hopes, and my imagination was thwarted in all its plans. Reflecting attentively on this, I thought that, if it were possible for me to take the feeling that impels me to love one individual and extend it to the entire sex which comprises the object of that emotion, I would procure new and intense pleasures for myself without in any way compromising myself. What reproach, indeed, could be addressed to a man who found himself equipped with a heart vigorous enough to love all the lovable women in the world? Yes, madam, I love them all, and not just those whom I know or hope to meet, but all of them who live on the face of the earth. More than that, I love all the women who have ever lived, and those who *will* live, not to mention the even greater number that my imagination draws out of non-being; all possible women, in short, are included within the vast circle of my affections.

By what unjust and bizarre whim would I restrict a heart such as mine within the narrow bourns of a single society? Indeed, why should I circumscribe its flight within the limits of a kingdom or even a republic?

Sitting at the foot of a tempest-tossed oak tree, a young Indian widow mingles her sighs with the sound of the unleashed winds. The weapons of the warrior she loved are hung over her head, and the mournful sound they make as they knock against one another recalls to her heart the memory of her past happiness. Meanwhile, lightning is flickering through the clouds, and its livid flashes are reflected in her motionless eyes. While the funeral pyre that is to consume her is raised, she awaits, alone, without consolation, in the stupor of despair, a horrible death, which a cruel prejudice has forced her to prefer above life.

What a sweet and melancholy pleasure is felt by a man of sensibility when he comes up to this unfortunate woman to console her! While I sit on the grass next to her, trying to dissuade her from this horrible sacrifice, and, mingling my sighs with her sighs and my tears with her tears, I attempt to distract her from her sorrows, the whole town rushes over to the home of Mme d'A***, whose husband has just died from an attack of apoplexy. She is also resolved not to survive her sad loss, and is insensible to the prayers of her friends; she is letting herself die of starvation – and ever since this morning, when this news was imprudently broken to her, the unhappy woman has eaten only a biscuit, and drunk only a little glass of Malaga. I give this sorrowing woman only the attention necessary for me not to infringe the laws of my universal system, and I soon leave her house, since I am by nature jealous, and don't want to compromise myself with a whole host of consolers, any more than with people whom it is all too easy to console.

Women who are beautiful but unhappy have particular rights over my heart, and the tribute of sensibility that I owe them does not weaken the interest I take in those who are happy. This disposition endows my pleasures with an infinite variety, and allows me to pass in turn from melancholy to gaiety, and from a sentimental state of repose to exultation.

Often, too, I devise love stories based on ancient history, and I erase entire lines from the old registers of destiny. How often have I stopped the homicidal hand of Virginius and saved the life of his unfortunate daughter, the victim of both an excessive crime and an excessive virtue![18] This incident fills me with terror every time it springs to my mind; I am not in the least surprised that it triggered a revolution.

I hope that sensible people, as well as compassionate souls, will be grateful that I sorted out this business amicably; and every man with some experience of the world will judge with me that, if the decemvir had been allowed to proceed, that passionate man would not have failed to do justice to Virginia's virtue: the parents would have become involved; father Virginius would eventually have been appeased, and marriage would have ensued, in accordance with all due legal form.

But what would have become of the unhappy abandoned lover? Well, for that matter, what did the lover gain from this murder? But since you are intent on growing misty-eyed at his fate, let me tell you, my dear Marie, that six months after Virginia's death, he was not only fully consoled, but very happily married, and that after having several children, he lost his wife and remarried, six weeks later, the widow of a tribune of the people. These hitherto unknown circumstances have been discovered and deciphered from a palimpsest manuscript in the Ambrosian Library by an Italian scholar of antiquity. They will, unfortunately, add yet another page to the abominable history – already far too long – of the Roman Republic.

24

Having saved the alluring Virginia, I modestly fend off her gratitude; and, still desirous of rendering a service to beautiful women, I take advantage of a rainy night to slip over and furtively open up the tomb of a young vestal, whom the Roman Senate has barbarically buried alive, because she allowed the sacred fire of Vesta to go out, or perhaps because she got slightly burnt on its flames. I walk in silence through the unfrequented streets of Rome, filled with the mellow inner charm that precedes good deeds, especially when they are not without danger. I take care to avoid the Capitol, for fear of waking the geese, and, slipping past the guards at the Porta Collina, I manage to reach the tomb in safety, without being spotted.

At the noise I make on lifting up the stone that covers it, the unfortunate woman lifts her dishevelled head from the damp ground of the vault. I see her, by the gleam of the sepulchral lamp, casting her wild eyes all around her: in her delirium, the wretched victim thinks she is already on the banks of the Cocytus[19].

'Oh, Minos!' she exclaims. 'Oh, inexorable judge! It is true: on earth, I loved in contravention of Vesta's strict laws. If the gods are as barbaric as men, open up before me the abyss of Tartarus! I loved, and I still love.'

'No, no, you are not yet in the realm of the dead; come, you poor woman, come back up to earth! Be born again to light and love!' Saying this, I seize her hand, already icy from the chill of the tomb; I lift her into my arms, I clasp her to my heart, and I finally drag her out of that dreadful place, while she shudders with alarm and gratitude.

Do not so much as imagine, madam, that any self-interest lay behind this good deed. The hope of arousing the lovely ex-vestal to take an interest in me played no part in what I had just done for her; had it done so, I would merely have relapsed into the old method; I can assure you – traveller's honour – that throughout our route, from the Porta Collina to the place where the tomb of the Scipios is now situated, in spite of the deep darkness, and even at the times when her weakness obliged me to hold her up in my arms, I never ceased to treat her with the regard and the respect due to her misfortunes, and I scrupulously restored her to her lover, who was awaiting her on the road.

25

Another time, as my daydreams led me along, I found myself by chance at the scene of the Rape of the Sabine women: I was most surprised to see that the Sabine men were reacting in quite a different way from that recounted in history. Understanding nothing of this brawl, I offered my protection to a fleeing woman; and I couldn't refrain from laughing when I heard a furious Sabine warrior crying out in despair, 'Immortal gods! Why didn't I bring *my* wife to the party?'

26

Apart from that half of the human race for which I feel such a strong affection – do I dare to tell you? Will anyone believe me? – my heart is endowed with such a capacity for tenderness that all living beings, and even inanimate things, also have their fair share of it. I love the trees that lend me their shade, and the birds twittering in the leaves, and the nocturnal hooting of the owl, and the roar of the torrents: I love everything… I love the moon!

You are laughing, miss – it's easy to poke fun at feelings that you don't share – but those hearts that are made like mine will understand me.

Yes, I am bound by the bonds of affection to everything that surrounds me. I love the paths I walk down, the fountain from which I drink: only with a certain twinge do I leave behind the branch that I picked up at random from a hedgerow; I still gaze at it even after I have thrown it away; we had already struck up an acquaintance: I am filled with nostalgia for the leaves that fall, and even the zephyr as it blows by. Where now is the man who stroked your black hair, Elisa, when, sitting next to you on the banks of the Doire, on the eve of our eternal separation, you gazed at me sadly and silently? Where is your gaze? Where is that moment, so painful and cherished?

O time! Dread deity! It is not your cruel scythe that fills me with terror; I fear only your hideous children, Indifference and Forgetfulness, who turn three-quarters of our lifespan into a long death.

Alas! This zephyr, this gaze, this smile are as far from now as the adventures of Ariadne: all that remains in the depths of my heart are regrets and empty memories; a melancholy brew, on which my life continues to swim, just as a vessel smashed by the tempest continues to float for a while on the stormy sea!…

27

Until, as the water slowly seeps in through the broken planks, the unhappy vessel disappears, swallowed up by the abyss; the waves sweep over it, the tempest calms down, and the sea swallow skims over the solitary and tranquil plain of the ocean.

28

I find myself forced, at this point, to bring to an end my explanation of my new way of making love, since I can see that it is falling on deaf ears. However, it will not be entirely irrelevant if I add a few more elucidations on the subject of this discovery, which does not generally suit everybody or every period of life. I wouldn't advise anyone to put it into practice at the age of twenty. The inventor himself didn't use it at that time of life. To derive the maximum benefit from it, you *do* need to have experienced all the sorrows of life without being discouraged, and all its pleasures without being sated. One difficulty: it is especially useful at that age when reason counsels us to give up the habits of youth, and may serve as an intermediary and an imperceptible passage between pleasure and wisdom. This passage, as all the moralists have observed, is extremely difficult. Few men have the noble courage to get through it with their heads held high; and often, having taken this step, they get bored on the other side, and step back over the ditch with grey hair, and overcome with shame. This is something they will avoid without pain thanks to my new way of making love. In fact, most of our pleasures are nothing but a whim of the imagination, and it is essential to present it with some innocent fodder so as to lure it away from the objects that we must give up, more or less in the same way that toys are presented to children when they aren't allowed to have sweeties. In this way, we have time to find our feet on the terrain of reason without even realising we are there yet, and we reach it along the path of madness, which will make access easier for a great many people.

So I don't think I was mistaken when I thought I could make myself useful by picking up my pen, and all I need to do now is to defend myself against the natural impulse of self-esteem that I might be justified in feeling by revealing such truths as these to mankind.

29

All these confidential remarks, my dear Sophie, will not have led you to forget, I hope, the embarrassing position you left me in, outside my window. The emotion that the sight of my neighbour's pretty little foot had filled me with was still intense, and I had more than ever fallen under the dangerous spell of that slipper, when an unforeseen event occurred that saved me from the peril I was in of falling from the fifth storey down into the street. A bat that had been fluttering round the house and that, on seeing me motionless for such a long time, apparently took me for a chimney, suddenly came diving down at me and fastened onto my ear. I felt on my cheek the horrid chill of its damp wings. All the echoes of Turin replied to the furious cry I uttered in spite of myself. The distant sentinels shouted, 'Who goes there?' and I heard in the street the quick march of a patrol.

I abandoned without much compunction my vista over the balcony, which no longer held much allure for me. The night's cold had seized me. A slight shudder ran from my head to my feet; and as I wrapped my dressing gown tightly round me to warm myself up, I saw, to my great regret, that this sensation of cold, together with the insult offered me by the bat, had been quite enough to change yet again the course of my ideas. The magical slipper would at this moment have had no more influence over me than the tresses of Berenice or any other constellation. I immediately calculated how unreasonable it would be to spend the night exposed to the inclemency of the weather, rather than to follow nature's promptings, which urge us to sleep. My reason, which at this moment was acting alone within me, led me to see this as proven – as rigorously as any proposition in Euclid. Finally, I was all at once deprived of imagination and enthusiasm, and delivered over to melancholy reality, without any right of appeal. Lamentable existence! One might as well be a dry tree in a forest, or an obelisk in the middle of a city square!

What two strange machines they are, I then exclaimed: the head and the heart of man! Swept away successively by these two forces that drive his actions, the last one he follows always seems to him to be the best! 'O madness of enthusiasm and feeling!' says frigid Reason. 'O weakness and uncertainty of reason!' says Feeling. Who will ever be able – or bold enough – to decide between them?

I thought it would be an excellent idea to discuss this question there and then, and to decide once and for all to which of these two guides I should entrust myself for the remainder of my life. Would I henceforth follow my head or my heart? Let's investigate.

30

As I said these words, I became aware of a dull pain in the foot that was resting on the rung of the ladder. I was, in addition, exhausted by the difficult position I had been maintaining until then. I gently lowered myself to sit down; and, leaving my legs to dangle to the left and right of the window, I started my journey on horseback. I have always preferred this way of travelling to all others, and I am passionately fond of horses; still, of all those I have seen, or those I have heard about, the one I would most ardently have wished to possess is the wooden horse which is spoken of in the *Thousand and One Nights*, on which you could travel through the air, and which sped off as fast as lightning when you turned a little peg between its ears.

Now, you may remark that my mount resembled a great deal the one mentioned in the *Thousand and One Nights.* Thanks to his position, the traveller, astraddle his window, communicates on the one side with the sky, and can enjoy the imposing spectacle of nature; meteors and stars are at his disposal: on the other side, the sight of his dwelling place and the objects that it contains bring him back to the idea of his existence, and make him turn his thoughts back to himself. A single movement of his head acts as a replacement for the enchanted peg, and is sufficient to bring about in the traveller's soul a change as rapid as it is extraordinary. One minute he is an inhabitant of the earth, the next of the heavens – and his heart and mind experience the full gamut of pleasures that it is granted man to feel.

I could anticipate in advance the full benefits I might derive from my steed. When I felt I was firmly and comfortably ensconced in the saddle, certain that I had nothing to fear from thieves or from my horse stumbling, I decided that this was a golden opportunity to turn to an investigation of the problem that I had to resolve, touching the pre-eminence of reason or feeling. But my first reflection on this subject made me stop in my tracks. 'Is it really for me to set myself up as a judge in a cause like this?' I murmured to myself – 'for me, who, within my conscience, have already decided in favour of feeling? – But on the other hand, if I exclude the people whose heart wins out over their head, whom will I be able to consult? A geometer? Pah! They're all in the pay of reason…' To decide this matter, I'd need to find a man who had received from nature an equal dose of reason and feeling, and at the moment of decision these two faculties would need to be in a state of perfect balance… which is quite impossible! It would be easier to establish a balance of power in a republic.

So the only competent judge would be one who had nothing in common with either of them – in other words, a man without either head or heart. This strange consequence made my reason rebel; my heart, in turn, protested that it had no part in it. And yet it seemed to me that I had reasoned it through correctly, and on this occasion I would have formed the worst possible idea of my intellectual faculties if I had not reflected that, in high metaphysical speculations such as the one in question, philosophers of the first rank have often been led, by sustained logical reasoning, to the most dreadful consequences, which have had their influence on the happiness of human society. So I consoled myself by thinking that the result of my speculations would at least not harm anyone. I left the question undecided, and I resolved, for the rest of my days, to follow alternatively either my head or my heart, depending on which of the two triumphed over the other. I really believe that this is the best method. It hasn't, admittedly, actually helped me to make much of a fortune up until now, I told myself. Never mind; I will carry on, making my way down life's swift path, without fear and without any plans for the future, laughing and crying in turn and often both at the same time, or else whistling some old tune to relieve my boredom as I make my way alone. At other times, I pick a daisy from some hedge corner; I pluck its leaves one after another, saying, 'She loves me a little, a lot, passionately, not at all.' The last one almost always produces a *not at all*. It's true: Elisa doesn't love me any more.

While I busy myself with these thoughts, the whole present generation of the living is passing by: like a great wave, it will soon, together with me, be breaking against the shores of eternity; and as if the storm of life were not impetuous enough, as if it pushed us too slowly up against the barriers of existence, the nations in their multitudes murder each other as they rush forward, and thereby forestall the term fixed by nature. Conquerors, themselves swept away by the swift whirlpool of time, amuse themselves by laying low thousands of men. Ah, gentlemen, what can you be thinking of? Wait!… these fine folk were going to die at their own pace. Can't you see the wave advancing? It is already foaming near the shore… Wait, in Heaven's name, for just one moment more, and it will all be up with you, and your enemies, and me, and the daisies! Such madness can never cease to astonish. Come now, that's one thing we can agree on; from now on, you won't catch *me* playing 'she loves me, she loves me not' with the daisies.

31

Having settled on a prudent rule of conduct for the future, thanks to a lucid and logical piece of reasoning, as we have seen in the preceding chapters, I was left with one highly important point to settle, on the subject of the journey I was about to undertake. It's not enough, after all, just to sit in a carriage or on a horse – you also need to know where you want to go. I was so tired by the metaphysical investigations with which I had just been busying myself that, before deciding to which region of the globe I would give my preference, I wanted to rest awhile and not think of anything. This is a way of existing which is also an invention of mine, and it has often been beneficial to me; but it isn't granted to everyone to make use of it: for while it may be easy to give your ideas a certain profundity by thinking attentively of a certain subject, it isn't easy to bring your thoughts to a halt all at once in the way you stop the pendulum of a clock. Molière was quite wrong to make fun of a man who spent his time spitting into a well to watch the circles he made in the water;[20] for my part, I am inclined to think that the man in question was a philosopher who had the power to suspend the action of his intelligence in order to rest – one of the most difficult operations that the human mind can perform. I know that the persons who have received this faculty without having wished for it, and who don't usually have a thought in their heads, will accuse me of plagiarism and will claim priority; but the state of intellectual immobility I have in mind is quite different from the one they enjoy, and for which M. Necker has composed an apologia.[21] Mine is always voluntary and can only be momentary; to enjoy it to the full, I closed my eyes and leant with both hands against the window, in the same way that a weary horseman leans on the pummel of his saddle, and soon the memory of the past, the sense of the present and the anticipation of the future were equally obliterated within my soul.

As this mode of existence powerfully encourages the invasion of sleep, after half a minute of pleasure, I felt my head falling onto my breast: I immediately opened my eyes, and my ideas reverted to their previous course – a circumstance which obviously proves that the kind of voluntary lethargy in question is quite different from sleep, since

I was awakened by sleep itself – something which has certainly never occurred to anyone else before.

Raising my eyes to the sky, I noticed the pole star over the rooftop of the house; this struck me as an excellent augury, coming just as I was about to set off on a long journey. During the interval of repose that I had just enjoyed, my imagination had regained all its strength, and my heart was ready to receive the most pleasant impressions – so much can this fleeting annihilation of thought increase its vigour! The basic feeling of sadness that my precarious situation in the world made me dimly feel was all at once replaced by an intense sense of hope and courage; I felt that I was capable of facing up to life and all the vicissitudes of misfortune or happiness that it brings in its train.

'Bright and shining star!' I exclaimed, in the delicious ecstasy that had ravished me, 'incomprehensible product of eternal thought! You who, alone, immobile in our eyes, have watched over half the earth since the first day of creation! You who guide the navigator over the deserts of the ocean – while a single glimpse of you has often restored hope and life to the sailor harried by the tempest! If it is true that, whenever a clear night has allowed me to contemplate the sky, I have never failed to seek you out from among your fellow-stars, assist me now, celestial light! Alas! Earth abandons me: be you today my counsellor and my guide, teach me in which region of the globe I must settle!'

During this invocation, the star seemed to shine more radiantly and to rejoice in the sky, inviting me to draw near to its protective influence.

I do not believe in presentiments; but I do believe in a divine providence which guides men by unknown means. Every instant of our existence is a new creation, the act of an omnipotent will. The inconstant order which produces the ever-new forms and the inexplicable phenomena of the clouds is determined, as regards every single moment, down to the most minute particle of water composing them: the events of our lives can have no other cause, and to attribute them to chance would be the height of folly. I can even affirm that it has sometimes been granted me to make out the imperceptible threads with which Providence manipulates great men like puppets, while they have the illusion that *they* are the ones conducting the world; a little impulse of pride whispered by Providence into their hearts is enough to make entire armies perish, and to turn a whole nation upside down. Be that as it may, I believed so strongly in the reality of the invitation that I had been given by the pole star that my mind was made up at that very moment; I was heading north; and although I had in those remote regions no point of preference or any definite aim in mind, when I left Turin the next day, I came out through the palace gate, which is to the north of the city, convinced that the pole star would not abandon me.

32

This was the point I had reached on my journey when I was obliged to get off my horse in rather a hurry. I wouldn't have mentioned this particular detail if I were not obliged in all conscience to instruct those people who would like to adopt this manner of travelling of the little drawbacks it involves, now that I have explained its immense advantages to them.

Since windows, in general, were not invented for the new purpose I have assigned to them, the architects who construct them neglect to give them the conveniently rounded form of a hunting saddle. The intelligent reader will, I hope, understand without any further explanation the painful cause that forced me to come to a halt. I climbed down, not without difficulty, and walked up and down the length of my room a few times to shake off the numbness, reflecting on the mixture of pleasures and pains that strew life's path, as well as on the kind of fate that renders men the slaves of the most insignificant circumstances. After this, I hastened to remount my horse, now provided with an eiderdown cushion – something I would never had dared to do a few days before, for fear of being jeered at by the cavalry; but since, the day before, I had at the gates of Turin met a band of Cossacks who had arrived on similar cushions from the borders of the Palus Maeotis and the Caspian Sea, I decided that I could, without infringing the laws of horsemanship – for which I have the greatest respect – adopt the same custom.

Delivered from the disagreeable sensation that I have intimated, I was able without any further worry to turn my thoughts to my planned journey.

One of the difficulties that was giving me the biggest headache, since it involved my conscience, was that of knowing whether I was doing the right thing or the wrong thing in abandoning my fatherland, half of which had indeed abandoned me. Such a step seemed too important for me to decide on lightly. As I reflected on the word 'fatherland', I realised that I didn't have a very clear idea of what it meant. 'My fatherland? In what does my fatherland consist? Could it just be a collection of houses, fields and rivers? That I can't believe. Perhaps it's my family and friends who constitute my fatherland? But they have already left it. I know – it's the government! But that has changed. Good Lord – so where *is* my fatherland?' I wiped my face with my hand in a state of unutterable anxiety. The love of one's fatherland is such a powerful emotion! The regrets that I myself felt at the mere thought of leaving mine proved to me so clearly the reality of this idea that I would have stayed on horseback all my life long rather than abandon the attempt to vanquish this difficulty.

I soon saw that the love of one's fatherland depends on a combination of several elements – in other words, on the way that over a long period of time man becomes accustomed, from childhood onwards, to individuals, his locality and the government. All I needed to do now was to investigate the extent to which these three basic factors contribute, each in their own way, to making up the fatherland.

Our attachment to our compatriots depends, in general, on the government, and is nothing other than the feeling of strength and happiness it gives us in common; for real attachment is limited to our family and to a small number of individuals by whom we are closely surrounded. Everything which gets in the way of our habit of meeting one another, or the ease with which we do so, makes men into enemies: a mountain range creates populations on either side that treat those on the other side as foreigners, and no longer love them; the people who dwell on the right bank of a river believe themselves to be quite superior to those on the left bank, and the latter in turn look down on their neighbours. This predisposition is evident even in big cities divided by a river, despite the bridges that yoke its banks. A difference of language separates men under the same government even more: finally, even the family, in which our real affections reside, is often scattered across the fatherland; it is continually changing in shape and number; furthermore, it can even be sent to live abroad. So it is neither in our compatriots nor in our family that love of fatherland essentially resides.

Locality contributes at least as much to the attachment we feel for our native land. A question of considerable interest arises in connection with this point: it has always been remarked how mountain dwellers are, of all peoples, the ones who are the most attached to their countries, and that nomads generally live in the great plains. So what can be the cause of this difference in the attachment of different peoples to their locality? Unless I am mistaken, the reason is this: in the mountains, your fatherland has a definite shape and character; in the plains, it has no such thing. It's a faceless woman, whom no one could love, whatever good qualities she might have. After all, what is left of his local country to the inhabitant of a wooden village, when that village is burnt down by the enemy passing through, and the trees all cut down? The unhappy man seeks in vain, all round the uniform line of the horizon, some recognisable object that can evoke some memories in him; but there is none. Every point of space presents the same appearance to him, and has the same interest. This man is a de facto nomad, unless his habitual attachment to his government keeps him where he is; but his dwelling place may be here or there, it makes no difference; his fatherland is wherever the government is active: he will have but half a fatherland. The mountain dweller is attached to the objects he has had in front of his eyes ever since childhood – objects that have visible and indestructible shapes: from every point in the valley, he can see and recognise his field on the mountainside. The noise of the torrent rushing down between the rocks is never interrupted; the path leading to the village takes a detour round an immovable block of granite. He sees in his daydreams the outline of the mountains, painted in his heart, just as, when you have gazed for a long time at a stained-glass window, you can still see it even when you close your eyes: the picture engraved in his memory is part of himself and will never be erased. Finally, even his memories are attached to his locality; but that locality must have objects whose origin is unknown, and whose end one cannot foresee. Ancient buildings, old bridges – everything that is imbued with a character of grandeur and durability can partly replace mountains and inspire in its own way a love of one's locality: nonetheless, the monuments of nature have more power over one's heart. To give Rome a worthy nickname, the proud Romans called it *the city on seven hills*. Once you have acquired a certain habit, it can never be destroyed. The mountain dweller, in his maturity, can no longer feel any affection for the localities of a big city, and the city dweller can never go and live in the mountains. This may explain why one of the greatest writers of our day, who has depicted with genius the deserts of America, has found the Alps quite unimpressive, and considers Mont Blanc to be much too small.[22]

The role played by the government is evident: it is the first basis of a fatherland. It is the government which creates a reciprocal attachment between men, and makes the attachment they naturally feel for their locality even more vigorous; it alone, by its memories of happiness or glory, can attach them to the soil that saw their birth.

Is the government good? Then the fatherland is at the height of its powers. Does it turn bad? Then the fatherland falls sick. Does it change? Then the fatherland dies. We then have a new fatherland, and anyone is free to adopt it or to choose another one.

When the whole population of Athens left that city at the behest of Themistocles,[23] did the Athenians abandon their fatherland, or did they take it along with them on their ships?

When Coriolanus…

Good Lord! What an argument I have got involved in! I'm forgetting that I'm sitting astraddle my window.

33

There was an old woman, a relative of mine, very witty – her conversation was always very interesting. But her memory, both inconstant and fertile, often led her to leap from one episode to the next, and from one digression to another, to such an extent that she was obliged to ask her listeners for their help: 'So what was it I was telling you about?' she would ask, and often her listeners too had forgotten, which plunged the whole assembly into indescribable perplexity. Now, it may have been noticed that the same thing often happens to me in my narrations, and I have to admit that, yes, the plan and order of my journey mimic exactly the plan and order of my aunt's conversations; but I'm not going to ask for anyone's assistance, since I've realised that my subject comes back of its own accord, and just when I am least expecting it.

34

The persons who will not feel able to approve of my analysis of the 'fatherland' should be informed that, for some time already, sleep had been overpowering me, despite my efforts to fight it off. However, I'm not at all sure now whether I really did go to sleep just then, and whether the extraordinary things that I am going to relate were the effect of a dream or of a supernatural vision.

I saw descending from the sky a brilliant cloud that gradually drew close to me, and was covering, as if in a transparent veil, a young woman of twenty-two to twenty-three years of age. I would seek in vain for expressions to describe the feelings that the sight of her aroused in me. Her face, shining with kindliness and benevolence, had the charm of the illusions of youth, and was sweet as dreams of the future; her eyes, her tranquil smile, all her features indeed, were the realisation of the ideal being that my heart had been seeking for so long, and that I had despairingly thought I would never meet.

As I gazed at her, in delight and ecstasy, I saw the pole star gleaming between the curls of her black hair, which the north wind gently lifted, and, at the same time, words of consolation made themselves heard. Words, I say? – No! rather the mysterious expression of a celestial mind revealing the future to my intelligence, while my senses were still in the shackles of sleep; it was a prophetic communication from the favourable star that I had just been invoking, and whose meaning I will attempt to express in a human language.

'Your trust in me will not be betrayed,' said a voice whose timbre resembled the sound of Aeolian harps. 'Look, here is the countryside that I have kept for you; here is the good to which men aspire – in vain, if they think that happiness is a matter of calculation, and ask from earth what can only be obtained from Heaven.' At these words, the meteor returned to the depths of the sky, and the aerial divinity was lost to sight amid the mists of the horizon; but as she left, she looked at me with an expression that filled my heart with hope and trust. Immediately, burning with an ardent desire to follow her, I spurred on my steed with all my strength; and as I had forgotten to put on spurs, my right heel struck the corner of a tile with such violence that the pain woke me up with a start.

35

This accident was of real benefit for the geological part of my journey, since it gave me the opportunity to find out exactly how high my room was above the layers of alluvium that form the soil on which the city of Turin is built.

My heart was racing violently, and I had just counted three and a half beats since the time I had spurred on my horse, when I heard the sound of my slipper that had fallen into the street, which – once the time taken by heavy bodies in their accelerated fall and the time needed by the sound waves of the air to rise from the street to my ears had both been calculated – gives the height of my window as ninety-four feet three inches and nine tenths of an inch from the level of the pavement in Turin – supposing that my heart, shaken by this dream, was beating a hundred and twenty times a minute, which cannot be far from the truth. It's purely for scientific reasons that I have made so bold as to mention my slipper after talking about the slipper of my lovely neighbour: so I warn you that this chapter is meant for scientists, and for them alone.

36

The bright vision I had just been vouchsafed made me feel all the more intensely, when I awoke, the full horror of the isolation in which I found myself. I looked around me, and all I could see were rooftops and chimney pots. Alas! Hanging from the fifth storey, between heaven and earth, surrounded by an ocean of regrets, desires and anxieties, I was clinging to life only thanks to the uncertain glimmer of hope: an imaginary support whose fragility I had experienced all too often. Doubt soon returned to my heart, still battered and bruised by life's disappointments, and I firmly believed that the pole star had been mocking me. This was an unjust and culpable mistrust, and the star punished me for it by making me wait for ten years! Oh, if only I could have foreseen then that all those promises would be fulfilled, and that one day I would again find on earth the adored being whose image I had merely glimpsed in the heavens! Dear Sophie, if only I had known that my happiness would surpass all my expectations!… But I mustn't run ahead of myself: I will return to my subject, unwilling as I am to reverse the strict methodical order which I am forcing myself to follow as I write the account of my journey.

37

The clock in the bell tower of St Philip's slowly rang out midnight. I counted each chime, one by one, and the last drew a sigh from me.

'So,' I said, 'another day has just detached itself from my life; and although the diminishing vibrations of the brassy sound are still ringing in my ears, the part of my journey which preceded midnight is already as far away from me as the voyages of Ulysses or Jason. In this abyss of the past, seconds and centuries last just as long; and does the future have any more reality?' They are two voids between which I find myself balanced as if on the cutting edge of a blade. It is true: time seems to me to be something so inconceivable that I am tempted to believe that it really doesn't exist, and that what we call 'time' is nothing more than a punishment of the mind.

I rejoiced to have come up with this definition of time, just as dark and obscure as time itself, when another clock chimed midnight, which gave me a disagreeable feeling. There is always a certain ill humour lurking in my mind when I am vainly occupied with some insoluble problem, and I found this second admonitory tolling of the bell really rather out of place for a philosopher like me. But I was *really* put out a few seconds later when I heard from afar a third church bell, that of the Capuchin monastery situated on the other side of the Po, chiming midnight, as if out of malice.

When my aunt wanted to summon an old chambermaid, a rather crusty character, of whom she was however very fond, she was too impatient to remain content with ringing the bell just once, but kept tugging away at the bell-pull until her servant appeared.

'Come on now, Mlle Branchet!'

And the latter, irritated at being forced to hurry like this, came ambling along, and replied with considerable sharpness before coming into the living room, 'I'm coming, I'm coming, madam!'

It was with a similar irritation that I heard the Capuchins' indiscreet bell chiming midnight for the third time.

'I know!' I cried, holding my hands out towards the clock; 'yes, I know, I *know* it's midnight: I know it all too well!'

There's no doubt about it: it was an insidious suggestion of the Evil

Spirit that led men to entrust the hours with the task of dividing up their days. Shut away in their dwelling places, they give themselves over to sleep or enjoyment, while each hour cuts one of the threads of their existence; the next day they merrily get up, not in the least suspecting that they have one more day. In vain does the prophetic brassy voice of the bell announce the approach of eternity, in vain does it repeat to them sadly every hour that goes by; they hear nothing, or, if they do hear, they do not understand. O midnight!... Dread hour!... I'm not superstitious, but this hour always filled me with a certain fear, and I have a premonition that, if I were ever to die, it would be at midnight. So – I *will* die one day? *I* will *die*? I – the person speaking, the person able to feel and touch myself – I might die? I find it rather difficult to believe: after all, others die, and there's nothing more natural than that: you see it happen every day: you see them passing away, you get used to it; but for you to die, you yourself – you in person! Well, that's a bit too much. And you, gentlemen, you who think that these reflections are a load of old nonsense, let me tell you that everyone thinks the same, you included! No one thinks that he is to die. If there were a race of immortal men, the idea of death would frighten them more than it does us.

There's something in all this that I can't quite understand. How is it that men, ceaselessly driven hither and thither by hope and by their illusory ideas about the future, are so little concerned by the one certain and inevitable event that the future holds in store for them? Might it be beneficent Nature herself that has given us this happy, carefree frame of mind, so that we can fulfil our destinies in peace? I do believe that you can be a perfectly decent fellow without adding to the real ills of life the cast of mind that leads you to brood over gloomy thoughts, and without your imagination being haunted by dark phantoms. In short, I think we should allow ourselves to laugh, or at least to smile, each time that an innocent opportunity to do so presents itself.

So concluded the meditation that the clock of St Philip's had inspired in me. I would have pursued it further if a certain scruple about the severity of the ethical code I had just established hadn't prevented me. But, not wishing to examine this doubt in any more detail, I whistled the tune of *Les Folies d'Espagne*[24], which has the property of changing the course of my ideas when they start heading off down the wrong track. The effect was so rapid that I immediately finished my ride on horseback.

38

Before going back into my room, I glanced over the city and the dark countryside around Turin that I was about to leave, perhaps for good, and I bade them a final farewell. Never had the night seemed so beautiful to me; never had the vista in front of my eyes struck me as so alluring. After saying goodbye to the mountain and the temple of Superga, I took my leave of the towers, the belfries, all the familiar objects that I had never imagined I would miss so intensely, and I took my leave too of the air and the sky, and of the river whose indistinct murmur seemed to reply to my farewell. Oh, if only I had been able to depict the feeling, tender and cruel at once, that filled my heart, and all the memories of the best half of my life hitherto, that came thronging in all around me like hobgoblins and tried to persuade me to stay in Turin! But alas, the memories of former happiness are like the wrinkles of the soul! When you're unhappy, you have to drive them from your thoughts like mocking phantoms which have come to insult your present condition: then it is a thousand times better to abandon yourself to the deceitful illusions of hope, and above all you need to put a brave face on a bad situation and take care you refrain from letting anyone in on the secret of your misfortunes. I have noticed, in the course of the ordinary journeys I have made among men, that if you go around being unhappy you end up making yourself ridiculous. At such dreadful moments, there's nothing that helps more than the new way of travelling that you have just been reading about. At this point, I experienced this in a decisive way: not only did I manage to forget the past, but also bravely to face up to my present difficulties. Time will sweep them away, I told myself, so as to give myself a bit of encouragement: time takes everything with it, and forgets nothing as it passes; and whether we try to arrest it, or push it forward, shoulder to the wheel, as they say, our efforts are equally in vain and change its invariable course not at all. Although I am generally not in the least worried by its swiftness, a particular circumstance or a particular association of ideas will remind me of it quite powerfully. It is when men fall silent, when the demon of noise is mute within its temple, in the midst of a sleeping city – it is then that Time raises its voice and makes itself heard within my soul. Silence and darkness become its interpreters, and reveal its mysterious march to me; it is no longer an abstract thing of reason that my thought cannot seize – my senses themselves perceive it. I can see it in the sky, chasing the stars westwards before it. Now it is pushing the rivers towards the sea, and rolling with the mist along the hillsides... I listen: the winds are moaning under the vigorous sweep of its swift wings, and the distant bell shudders at its terrible passage.

'Let us make the most of its forward momentum!' I exclaimed. 'I want to put the moments it will snatch from me to good use.' – Intent on putting this good resolution into practice, that very same moment, I leant forward to launch myself bravely onto the pathway, making with my tongue that clucking noise that has always been used to urge horses onwards, but that is impossible for me to write out in accordance with the rules of spelling:

'gh! gh! gh!'

and I finished my excursion on horseback with a sudden canter.

39

I was lifting my right foot to get down, when I felt someone hitting me quite roughly on the shoulder. To say that I was not alarmed at this incident would be to distort the truth; and this is the occasion to point out to the reader and to prove to him, without too much vanity, how difficult it would be for anyone other than me to carry out such a journey. Even supposing that the new traveller had a thousand times more means and talent for observation than I can ever have, could he ever hope to meet with such strange adventures, and so many of them, as those which have befallen me in the space of four hours, and which are clearly laid down by my destiny? If anyone doubts this, let him try to guess who had just hit me.

In the first moment of my alarm, not really thinking of the situation in which I found myself, I thought that my horse had kicked out or had dashed me against a tree. God knows how many dismal ideas came flooding into my mind during the short period of time it took me to turn my head and look into my room. I then saw, as often happens in the things that appear most extraordinary, that the cause of my surprise was perfectly natural. The same gust of wind which, at the start of my journey, had opened my window and slammed my door shut as it swept by, and part of which had slipped between the curtains round my bed, had just entered my room in great uproar. It flung the door open and went out through the window, pushing the pane against my shoulder – which caused the surprise I have just mentioned.

You will recall that it was on the invitation that this gust of wind had issued to me that I had left my bed. The shock I had just been given was quite obviously an invitation to go back to bed, and I felt I was obliged to accept this invitation. It is a fine thing, no doubt, to be on such a familiar terms with the night, the sky and its meteors, and to be able to derive benefit from their influence. Ah! The relations one is forced to have with men are much more dangerous! How often have I been the dupe of the trust I have placed in those gentlemen! I even had a few things to say about this in a note that I have omitted, since it turned out to be longer than the whole text, which would have distorted the proper proportions of my journey, whose small volume is its greatest merit.

NOTES

1. The Comte de Buffon (1701–88), author of a major work on natural history, was the most celebrated French scientist of his day.
2. The Doire is a tributary of the Po.
3. Hipparchus (d. after 127 BC) was a Greek astronomer who discovered the precession of the equinoxes.
4. Asti (the home of Asti spumante) is a town about forty-five kilometres south-east of Turin.
5. Lycurgus (seventh century BC) was a legendary Spartan lawgiver.
6. The Basilica of Superga is an early eighteenth-century church on a homonymous hill overlooking Turin.
7. i.e. Alexander Pope (1688–1744), the poet.
8. This is a pastiche of the language of Ossian/Macpherson.
9. 'He's crazy, by Bacchus, he's crazy!' (Italian).
10. Archytas of Tarentum (fl. *c*.400 BC) was a Pythagorean philosopher and inventor. His mechanical dove attracted the snobbish scorn of Plato.
11. The Battle of Fontenoy (1745) was a French victory in the War of the Austrian Succession.
12. Franz Joseph Gall (1758–1828) was a phrenologist who saw cranial 'bumps' as indicative of personal dispositions and talents.
13. See note 20 to *A Journey around my Room*. The 1839 edition here added this note: 'The author has not kept his word, and if anything has actually appeared under this title, the author of *A Journey around my Room* declares that he has absolutely nothing to do with it.'
14. Scapin and Jocrisse are bumptious figures in French comedy.
15. Zénéide was Princess Zinaida Volkonskaya (1793–1862), poet, playwright and translator, renowned for her lovely singing voice.
16. Tartarus, originally an abyss far below Hades, the Greek underworld, eventually became identified with Hell. The Styx was one of its rivers.
17. Praxiteles (370–330 BC) was a great Athenian sculptor.
18. Virginia was killed by her father Virginius (*c*.450 BC) to prevent her being dishonoured by one of the decemvirs (a board of ten patrician men), Appius Claudius. The logic of de Maistre's historical speculations is rather difficult to disentangle, but the main point is the humanitarian zeal to rewrite history.
19. Cocytus, another river in the Greek underworld.
20. Molière's play *Le Misanthrope* (1666) has a Viscount whiling away the time for three quarters of an hour by spitting into a well and watching the circles widen (Act V, scene 4).
21. Jacques Necker (1732–1804) was a prominent French politician who, as finance minister, was first recalled by Louis XVI to solve the problem of France's bankruptcy (1788) and then, when the Court became alarmed at his attempted solutions, dismissed (11th July 1789), one of the actions that precipitated the storming of the Bastille.

22. A reference to the much-travelled romantic writer François René Chateaubriand (1768–1848).
23. Themistocles (*c.*524–*c.*459 BC), famous Athenian statesman, democrat and commander of the fleet that beat the Persians at Salamis. He persuaded the Athenians to abandon their city temporarily to the Persians.
24. *Les Folies d'Espagne* was the title of several popular pieces of music by Marin Marais (1656–1728) and Jean-Baptiste Lully (1632–87), among others.

BIOGRAPHICAL NOTE

Xavier de Maistre was born in Chambéry, Savoy, in 1763 to French parents. He was one of ten children, his elder brother being the philosophical writer Comte Joseph-Marie de Maistre (1753–1821). Though fascinated by art and literature, de Maistre embarked upon a military career, and was serving in the Sardinian Army when Savoy was repatriated to France in 1792.

As a young officer in Piedmont he was arrested for duelling, and was sentenced to remain in his room for forty-two days. This 'imprisonment' resulted in his first work, *Voyage autour de ma chambre* [*A Journey around my Room*]. The manuscript was read by his brother Joseph, who arranged for its printing in 1795. Some years later he returned to the story and produced *Expédition nocturne autour de ma chambre* [*A Nocturnal Expedition around my Room*] (1825). This 'sequel' was told in a similar vein, and the two form a delightful parody of the travel literature of the time.

In 1799 de Maistre was serving in the Austro-Russian Army in Italy, but was forced to supplement his income with painting. His fortunes changed when Joseph was appointed envoy extraordinary to the King of Sardinia. De Maistre was given the position of librarian to the Admiralty Museum, from which point his military career advanced rapidly, and, after having fought in the Caucasian War, he rose to the position of general. He married a lady-in-waiting to the Empress and from that time on considered himself Russian.

Though not a prolific writer, de Maistre published two novels during his lifetime: *Les Prisonniers du Caucase* [*The Prisoners of the Caucasus*] and *La jeune Sibérienne* [*The Young Siberian Woman*]. He also penned a short dialogue, *Le Lépreux de la cité d'Aoste*. After a brief stay in Paris in 1839, he returned to St Petersburg, where he remained until his death in 1852.

Andrew Brown studied at the University of Cambridge, where he taught French for many years. He now works as a freelance teacher and translator. He is the author of *Roland Barthes: the Figures of Writing* (OUP, 1993), and his translations include *Memoirs of a Madman* by Gustave Flaubert, *For a Night of Love* by Emile Zola, *The Jinx* by Théophile Gautier, *Mademoiselle de Scudéri* by E.T.A. Hoffmann, *Theseus* by André Gide, *Incest* by Marquis de Sade, *The Ghost-seer* by Friedrich von Schiller, *Colonel Chabert* by Honoré de Balzac, *Memoirs of an Egotist* by Stendhal, *Butterball* by Guy de Maupassant and *With the Flow* by Joris-Karl Huysmans, all published by Hesperus Press.

HESPERUS PRESS CLASSICS

Hesperus Press, as suggested by the Latin motto, is committed to bringing near what is far – far both in space and time. Works written by the greatest authors, and unjustly neglected or simply little known in the English-speaking world, are made accessible through new translations and a completely fresh editorial approach. Through these classic works, the reader is introduced to the greatest writers from all times and all cultures.

For more information on Hesperus Press, please visit our website: **www.hesperuspress.com**

ET REMOTISSIMA PROPE

SELECTED TITLES FROM HESPERUS PRESS

George Eliot	*Amos Barton*	Matthew Sweet
Henry Fielding	*Jonathan Wild the Great*	Peter Ackroyd
F. Scott Fitzgerald	*The Popular Girl*	Helen Dunmore
Gustave Flaubert	*Memoirs of a Madman*	Germaine Greer
Ugo Foscolo	*Last Letters of Jacopo Ortis*	Valerio Massimo Manfredi
Elizabeth Gaskell	*Lois the Witch*	Jenny Uglow
Théophile Gautier	*The Jinx*	Gilbert Adair
André Gide	*Theseus*	
Johann Wolfgang von Goethe	*The Man of Fifty*	A.S. Byatt
Nikolai Gogol	*The Squabble*	Patrick McCabe
E.T.A. Hoffmann	*Mademoiselle de Scudéri*	Gilbert Adair
Victor Hugo	*The Last Day of a Condemned Man*	Libby Purves
Joris-Karl Huysmans	*With the Flow*	Simon Callow
Henry James	*In the Cage*	Libby Purves
Franz Kafka	*Metamorphosis*	Martin Jarvis
Franz Kafka	*The Trial*	Zadie Smith
John Keats	*Fugitive Poems*	Andrew Motion
Heinrich von Kleist	*The Marquise of O–*	Andrew Miller
Mikhail Lermontov	*A Hero of Our Time*	Doris Lessing
Nikolai Leskov	*Lady Macbeth of Mtsensk*	Gilbert Adair
Carlo Levi	*Words are Stones*	Anita Desai
Xavier de Maistre	*A Journey Around my Room*	Alain de Botton
André Malraux	*The Way of the Kings*	Rachel Seiffert
Katherine Mansfield	*Prelude*	William Boyd
Edgar Lee Masters	*Spoon River Anthology*	Shena Mackay
Guy de Maupassant	*Butterball*	Germaine Greer
Prosper Mérimée	*Carmen*	Philip Pullman
Sir Thomas More	*The History of King Richard III*	Sister Wendy Beckett
Sándor Petőfi	*John the Valiant*	George Szirtes

Francis Petrarch	*My Secret Book*	Germaine Greer
Luigi Pirandello	*Loveless Love*	
Edgar Allan Poe	*Eureka*	Sir Patrick Moore
Alexander Pope	*The Rape of the Lock* and *A Key to the Lock*	Peter Ackroyd
Antoine-François Prévost	*Manon Lescaut*	Germaine Greer
Marcel Proust	*Pleasures and Days*	A.N. Wilson
Alexander Pushkin	*Dubrovsky*	Patrick Neate
Alexander Pushkin	*Ruslan and Lyudmila*	Colm Tóibín
François Rabelais	*Pantagruel*	Paul Bailey
François Rabelais	*Gargantua*	Paul Bailey
Christina Rossetti	*Commonplace*	Andrew Motion
George Sand	*The Devil's Pool*	Victoria Glendinning
Jean-Paul Sartre	*The Wall*	Justin Cartwright
Friedrich von Schiller	*The Ghost-seer*	Martin Jarvis
Mary Shelley	*Transformation*	
Percy Bysshe Shelley	*Zastrozzi*	Germaine Greer
Stendhal	*Memoirs of an Egotist*	Doris Lessing
Robert Louis Stevenson	*Dr Jekyll and Mr Hyde*	Helen Dunmore
Theodor Storm	*The Lake of the Bees*	Alan Sillitoe
Leo Tolstoy	*The Death of Ivan Ilych*	
Leo Tolstoy	*Hadji Murat*	Colm Tóibín
Ivan Turgenev	*Faust*	Simon Callow
Mark Twain	*The Diary of Adam and Eve*	John Updike
Mark Twain	*Tom Sawyer, Detective*	
Oscar Wilde	*The Portrait of Mr W.H.*	Peter Ackroyd
Virginia Woolf	*Carlyle's House and Other Sketches*	Doris Lessing
Virginia Woolf	*Monday or Tuesday*	Scarlett Thomas
Emile Zola	*For a Night of Love*	A.N. Wilson